Janet Maughan

The Co-Heiress

A novel. Part 2

Janet Maughan

The Co-Heiress
A novel. Part 2

ISBN/EAN: 9783337050887

Printed in Europe, USA, Canada, Australia, Japan

Cover: Foto ©Andreas Hilbeck / pixelio.de

More available books at **www.hansebooks.com**

THE CO-HEIRESS.

A Novel.

BY THE

AUTHOR OF "CHARLEY NUGENT," AND

"ST. AUBYNS OF ST. AUBYN."

IN THREE VOLUMES.

VOL. II.

LONDON:

TINSLEY BROTHERS, CATHERINE STREET, STRAND.

1866.

LONDON:
SAVILL AND EDWARDS, PRINTERS, CHANDOS STREET,
COVENT GARDEN.

CONTENTS

OF

THE SECOND VOLUME.

THE CO-HEIRESS.

CHAPTER I.

ROMAN GOSSIP.

WE have before spoken of Count Salvi. Young, handsome, accomplished, and a member of a noble Roman family, he moved, as he was entitled to do, in the first circles both of the Italian and the English society, and was on an intimate footing in the house of Sir John de Burgh. Rich in lineage and ancestral dignities, he was but slenderly endowed in purse; and a wealthy marriage, if such were feasible, appeared to him the easiest solution of his difficulties; for indeed he found it no light matter to maintain an appearance befitting his rank and the society in which he moved. He had become acquainted with the De Burghs during their residence in Nice, and had been a frequent and welcome visitor; his agreeable conversational qualities and his great musical talents rendering his society highly acceptable both to Sir John and to his daughter.

Much as Count Salvi admired the grace and beauty of Miss de Burgh, and greatly as he estimated his privilege in being permitted to assist the young lady in the prosecution of her musical studies, her fame as a wealthy heiress formed no inconsiderable portion of her attraction in his eyes; and no long period of time had elapsed before the impoverished Italian noble had formed the design of restoring vigour to his slender finances by a union with the English baronet's daughter. He was sufficiently astute to be aware that there were some few difficulties in the way; differences in nationality and creed, as well as the slight obstacle of his fortune not being such as to render him a peculiarly desirable son-in-law to a calculating British parent. But here he imagined his really high rank would stand him in good stead; for as he knew the Englishman's regard for a satisfactory balance-sheet, he also appreciated the wonderful reverence for a title inherent in the breast of the true John Bull.

He fancied that to see his daughter Countess Salvi, Sir John de Burgh would be inclined to overlook the fact that her countess-ship would be little more than an empty name; he also trusted a good deal in the resolute character of the young lady herself, for the count was not slow to perceive that Augusta had a will of her own, and a pretty strong one.

If she were once on his side, and her feelings interested in his favour, then Count Salvi believed the day must eventually be his; for he had taken some pains to ascertain that Miss de Burgh must under all circumstances inherit large property in her own right, entirely beyond her father's control. But he felt his way very cautiously; and determined to bide his time, and venture on no step till he was well assured of his position.

Until the arrival of Sir Charles Belling-

ham in Rome, he apparently had the field
entirely to himself; no other man, either a
foreigner or an Englishman, having the same
facilities of intercourse with Miss de Burgh,
and none certainly occupying the same
evidently favourable situation in her
regard.

But when the young English baronet
appeared on the scene, all this was changed;
and no one more speedily perceived the
great alteration that had taken place than
Count Salvi himself, blighting as it did
all his long-cherished hopes, and utterly
destroying the plans he had been so cautiously and carefully maturing. His fierce
Italian nature was roused to hate and
bitterness. In the early days of Roman
intrigue, Sir Charles Bellingham would
have paid dearly for his unconscious interference with the plans of his rival; but the
dagger and the bowl being now tolerably
obsolete, Count Salvi had no very ready
way of expressing his feelings of ven-
geance, and was compelled to restrain his
emotions of indignation and disgust, and

only give them free vent when alone and unobserved.

But the wily Italian soon perceived that in an active point of view Sir Charles could in no respect be considered as a rival; it became plain to his watchful observation that the young baronet had no particular design in his attentions to Miss de Burgh— but he saw that she loved the young Englishman, and he thought it more than probable that, though at present apparently indifferent to her regard, Sir Charles might in time be brought to reciprocate it. He was well aware of Miss de Burgh's feelings as respected Emily Crewe: her dislike to and jealousy of that young lady were no secret to him, and more than once he had sought to make them subservient to his own ends.

But as yet he had ventured on no step of a decisive nature, having been content to remain a silent spectator of events, biding the arrival of the time when it should seem to him that his interference might be useful or necessary; and at this point we now find him.

On coming back from her drive with Lady Agnes Bellingham, Miss de Burgh found that her father had been out for a short time, but had already returned to the house. When she entered the *salon* he was pacing the apartment with an impatient step, and his countenance wore an expression of haughty displeasure.

"I have been expecting your return for some time," he said, coldly; "I wish to have some conversation with you. Be seated, if you please."

Augusta obeyed him in silence.

" I have been much annoyed this afternoon," said Sir John, after a moment's pause; "very much annoyed, indeed."

"I am sorry to hear it," replied his daughter, calmly.

" You do not inquire the cause!"

"Have I anything to do with it?" said Augusta; "for, if so, I am in perfect ignorance of what it can be. I do not imagine you were seriously annoyed at my driving with Lady Agnes Bellingham."

" You were not alone with her; her son was with you, too."

" Certainly he was," replied Augusta, striving hard to restrain a rising blush; " I was not consulted as to his being of the party, and should never have dreamt of objecting if I had been."

" Probably not," said her father, in a tone of sarcasm; " in fact, you would most likely have preferred his being there."

" I think I should," replied Augusta, with perfect calmness; " Sir Charles is very agreeable; his conversation made the time pass very pleasantly."

" No doubt of it, Miss de Burgh—no doubt of it. But pleasure may sometimes be too dearly bought; at the price of honour and good name, for example."

" I do not understand you, papa." She looked him full in the face as she spoke. There was no shrinking or timidity in her pale but resolute countenance. No conduct of mine merits language such as this."

" You think not!" said Sir John, bitterly; " do you know that your folly is the talk— the jest of all Rome ?"

"Papa!" and Augusta half rose from her seat with indignation; "what *do* you mean?"

"I mean that my daughter, Miss de Burgh, the heiress of a name that might lead her to feel some little pride and self-respect, has by her behaviour laid herself open to remarks that would insult a peasant."

Augusta's brow grew very black, and one small hand was firmly clenched; but she ventured no observation, and only sat sternly regarding her father.

"Do you know what they have dared to say about you?" continued Sir John, with kindling wrath; "that you, the heiress of the De Burghs, are throwing yourself openly and unblushingly at the head of a man who uses you but as a pastime—as the amusement of a leisure hour! That everyone, himself included, is aware of your partiality for him; and it is fully believed, that should he amiably resolve to have compassion on you, and offer you the name of Lady Bellingham, your delighted acceptance is to be looked upon as a matter of course! This is said of *my* daughter!" He ad-

vanced a step towards her as she sat there,
and looked fiercely into her face as if de-
manding an answer.

" It is false," said Augusta, from between
her firmly-compressed lips.

" It is said, however," replied her father,
with a sneer; " and your precious friend,
Miss Crewe, is said to be another claimant
for the honour, with a chance fully equal
to your own. Perhaps you will tell me
which side I had better back."

" Where did you learn all this, papa?"
said Augusta, quietly.

" It does not matter," replied her father;
" I overheard a remark not intended for my
ear, and one sufficiently plain to apprise
me of the state of the case."

" And you believed all you heard. You
have had much opportunity of judging;
have you ever seen anything in me that
should lead you to suppose me wanting in
self-respect?"

Her calmness rather staggered Sir John.

" I cannot say that I have," he replied;
" but I have not been always with you."

" My conduct is at all times the same," said Augusta, with composure; " I have no reason to court concealment, and I have never done so. What every one has seen you have also seen, and you can form a just conclusion for yourself."

" Why, then, are such remarks made?" persisted her father; " they must surely have some foundation."

"Tattlers and busybodies are everywhere," replied Augusta; "and in Rome they are not absent. Was any especial enormity laid to my charge? Our intimacy with Lady Agnes Bellingham and her son is an acknowledged fact; there was nothing so very marked in the circumstance of my driving with her."

" In the opinion of those whose remarks I overheard, it was looked on as a positive confirmation of their suppositions. I do not choose my daughter to be exposed to such comments; therefore I must beg that for the future you will so order your conduct that they shall cease. If not, I shall feel under the necessity of quitting Rome."

Augusta felt her heart die within her as he spoke those words. But she replied, composedly, " You have warned me, papa, and I shall be careful. I cannot answer that no remarks will be made, for gossip is beyond all possibility of control; but at any rate I shall have given no occasion for them."

" I shall trust you," said Sir John, more kindly than he had hitherto spoken; " I have always done so, Augusta."

" Are Sir Charles Bellingham's attentions such as to call for any particular comment?" observed Sir John, after a short pause. " He has been very much in our society since we have been in Rome: has this report any shadow of foundation ?"

" His attentions are such as any gentleman may offer to a lady," replied Augusta, striving to speak calmly; " his manner is very much alike to every one. He is very intimate with Mrs. Greville and her sister. I think you said Miss Crewe's name was also mentioned equally flatteringly with my own."

" It was: and that annoyed me beyond

measure. Miss Crewe is a handsome girl undoubtedly; very agreeable and accomplished, and a thorough lady; but she does not hold your position, Augusta. I look high for you, Augusta, though I have hitherto in no way interfered with your selection. You have been free to please yourself, because I felt sure that in so doing you would also please me."

"When the time comes, if it ever does so, papa, I hope we shall neither of us have any cause to be ashamed of my choice."

"I hope not, Augusta: indeed, I may say I think not. I shall rely on your discretion for the future. I regret that in the heat of my indignation I perhaps spoke with rather unwarrantable force. I felt decidedly angry, having been much annoyed by the whole affair."

"You had some reason," replied his daughter, rising from the sofa on which she had been seated, "but I trust it is all ended now, and hope there may be no occasion to revert to the subject. I believe I must leave you now. We dine at Lord

A——'s you know, and I shall require all the time left for dressing."

She accordingly quitted the room and proceeded to her own apartments, where she found she had indeed little more than the ordinary time for preparation. Therefore, though she longed to be alone and able to reflect calmly on all that had passed, any indulgence in solitary meditation was for the present impossible.

Summoning her maid for the important duties of the toilette, Augusta resigned herself into her hands; but while the woman was brushing and arranging the long silky tresses of her young mistress, that mistress leant back in her chair pondering gravely and anxiously on all she had heard; deep shadows of thought coming into the beautiful countenance, deep lines of care into the smooth white forehead.

Was it then true? Had her feelings, her miserable but unconquerable weakness for this man been the observation, the talk of all Rome? Had she, the descendant of the haughty race of De Burgh, indeed sunk so low as this? A heavy frown crossed her throbbing brow, and her maid glancing at her mistress in the mirror just opposite, marvelled greatly what cause brought so gloomy an expression into the face of one who, to her ignorant eyes, seemed at the very summit and crown of earthly felicity.

As on a former occasion she gazed at herself in the mirror when fully dressed, and calmly scrutinized her wondrous loveliness, that gift of rare price which so many praised and so many envied.

"Ah!" she thought, sorrowfully, "how little has it done for me! What has it brought me that I care for? Admiration, jealousy perhaps; but no love. I would give it all for true love; for that love an hour of which I would win at the sacrifice of life itself." Thus bitterly reflecting she turned slowly away and proceeded to join her father; the carriage was already at the door, and they immediately started for the party at Lord A——'s.

CHAPTER II.

THE party at Lord A——'s was to be a very gay one; a large dinner party first, and an assemblage of evening guests afterwards.

Augusta was richly attired in a dress of costly lace, looped up and decorated with crimson camellias, one lovely flower and bud of the same in her hair.

As she entered the room leaning on her father's arm, a subdued murmur might be distinguished passing round the circle. More than one handsome woman was present, Lady A—— herself was young and beautiful, but Miss de Burgh shone pre-eminent among them all, her father and herself forming a couple but rarely equalled even among the highest ranks of the English aristocracy.

Among the arrivals after dinner — the dinner was a very pleasant one—were Mrs. Greville and Miss Crewe, and Sir Charles Bellingham.

When the latter entered the room, he almost directly came up to where Augusta was sitting, and placed himself on the ottoman beside her. She saw many observant glances turned towards them, and guessed what remarks were probably being made ; Sir John de Burgh stood at a little distance, talking to Lord A——, but, though apparently fully engrossed by him, Augusta felt that his eye was upon her, and that he was carefully noting her every look and action. Carelessly extending her hand to Sir Charles, she gave an indifferent reply to his salutation, and then fell languidly back against the cushions of the ottoman.

Her manner was so different from what it had been in the earlier part of the day, that Sir Charles glanced at her with a slight feeling of surprise. He thought she looked paler than usual, and there was an unwonted gravity in her expression; so bending eagerly forward, he inquired with kind anxiety if she felt fatigued.

"A little," replied Augusta, quietly, and in such a languid tone that Sir Charles at once concluded she was really ill.

"You have not a comfortable seat there," he said, as he again bent forward; "it is too much in the glare of the light. May I not find you another better placed?"

"I do not wish to move, thank you," replied Augusta; "I am very well where I am."

She had never spoken to him like this before, and he scarcely knew what to make of it.

While he was debating in his mind any imaginable cause for her now evident coldness, so utterly different from all his previous experience of her manner to himself, Sir John de Burgh ended his conversation with Lord A——, and approached the place where his daughter was sitting.

He accosted Sir Charles, who stood silently by Augusta, but his greeting had a certain stiffness that was not unperceived by the young baronet. "What on earth have I done?" was his inward reflection; "nothing that I can possibly call to mind—yet surely there must be some reason for Miss de Burgh's reserve and her father's dryness. We were the best friends imaginable this morning; what can have happened since?"

"Augusta," said Sir John, after his brief salutation to Sir Charles, "Lord A—— has just mentioned that there are some remarkably fine flowers in the conservatory, and I wish you to come with me now and look at them."

Miss de Burgh rose at once and took her father's arm. On another occasion Sir Charles would have readily accompanied them; but now he paused, for the manner of both was such as to make him think that they did not care for his company. "I must find out what it is all about," he soliloquised, as he watched their progress across the crowded room. "Something is decidedly wrong; but most assuredly I have no idea what it is."

So saying he threaded his way among the guests, and presently stumbled on Miss Crewe and her sister sitting by an open window, which admitted the perfume of some rare plants from the terrace just outside. They were not alone, for various adorers of the fair Emily hovered round them; but when Miss Crewe perceived Sir Charles Bellingham, a beaming smile irradiated her countenance, and she frankly and unhesitatingly made room for him near herself; a warning glance from Norah having no effect whatever in checking the cordial impulse of the warm-hearted Irish girl.

This was considerably pleasanter than the coldness of Miss de Burgh, and Sir Charles accepted the seat accorded to him with entire contentment, and speedily ceased to reflect on the circumstances of the previous quarter of an hour.

"How charming the parties here are!" said Emily, after a pause, during which they had listened with great enjoyment to a brilliant performer on the piano; "no formality, no stiffness, no *gêne*, as is almost always the case at similar entertainments in our own beloved England. There, somehow, nearly all our social meetings bore one past description—dinners, dances, concerts, they are all alike—the most fatiguing, wearisome things possible."

"And yet you contrived to go to a good many, my dear," retorted her sister, laughing; "and sometimes you looked as though you had not found them so very stupid after all."

"And I must be allowed to express a doubt as to any party being either wearisome or formal where Miss Crewe was present," added Sir Charles Bellingham. "I shall never forget the evening I first had the supreme felicity of meeting you and your sister. Your entrance was the signal for all dark shadows to disperse from that previously awful party. I remember I had just been meditating what enormous misdeed of mine could have brought on me such condign punishment as I was then reluctantly enduring, when the door was opened, and——"

" A dazzling vision of light and loveliness flooded the room with sunshine," said Miss Crewe, laughingly interrupting him. " I recollect the party quite well—at old Lady South's it was : the stingiest, most disagreeable old woman in all London. Her ices might have lain in a teaspoon, and her maccaroons were at least a month old. What dreary parties hers were! fatiguing both to mind and body. I can't think how I ever consented to go to them."

" Don't abuse, at least, that particular one," replied Sir Charles, " when I am recalling it with such touching tenderness as an oasis in the desert of London society. You sang; and on that evening I experienced a new sensation."

Lady A—— at this moment entered the *salon* in which they were seated, and was evidently directing her course towards their corner.

" I come with a petition, Miss Crewe," said Lady A——, approaching her; " will you favour us with a song ? One of your charming ballads, of which I have heard so much.   Will you come further into the room?" she suggested, for they were sitting in what had once been a kind of alcove separated by an archway from the principal *salon*.   " Your voice would be greatly lost here ; and where is your guitar—for I believe that is your favourite instrument?"

"I have not brought it," replied Miss Crewe; "I did not feel sure of its being required; but it 'matters little, I am very independent, and can sing without any accompaniment at all."

She rose from the sofa as she spoke, and took up a position close to the archway, half leaning on a richly carved antique chair that stood conveniently near.   Next moment the exquisite melody of the " Last Rose of Summer" rose sweet and clear over the murmur of voices, hushing all other sounds in an instant, and holding the assemblage silent and, as it were, spellbound by the wonderful charm of the performance.   There was neither boldness nor affectation visible in the manner of Miss Crewe, though there were not wanting those who characterized it as partaking largely of both qualities; but such detractors were chiefly young ladies, unable or not choosing to sing themselves, and yet envious of the admiration bestowed on the handsome Irish girl, and jealous of the sensation created by her lovely voice, which they had not the generosity to enjoy or praise. Loud applause awaited the conclusion of the song, and Lady A——— warmly thanked Miss Crewe for the pleasure she had afforded them. Her ladyship remained for a short time in conversation with the fair singer and Sir Charles Bellingham, and then expressed a hope that Miss de Burgh might also be prevailed on to favour them with one of her charming Italian arias.

"Her style and yours are so different," she remarked to Emily, "that each is a charming contrast to the other, and almost sheds on it an additional beauty. Do you know where she is? for I have not seen her very lately."

"I believe she is in the conservatory," replied Sir Charles; "Sir John came for her a short time ago, saying he wished to show her some particular plants."

"Then, will you kindly convey my message to her?" said Lady A——. "I am wanted elsewhere, or I should go myself. If she will come in a few minutes, I shall be waiting for her at the piano."

Before he had made up his mind what to reply, she was gone; and nothing remained for the young baronet but obedience to the commands of his hostess.

"What is the matter?" inquired Emily, with a smile; for Sir Charles looked rather unwilling to perform the commission required of him, and his countenance wore an expression of doubtfulness.

"The truth is," he replied, after a moment's hesitation, "I don't quite like conveying this message of Lady A——'s to Miss de Burgh; and I wish she had just asked her to sing herself."

"Anything wrong?" said Miss Crewe, slightly arching her eyebrows.

"I don't see how there can be," replied Sir Charles; "but when I went up to speak to Miss de Burgh this evening, her manner was dry and indifferent—altogether the reverse of what it usually is.   At first I imagined it might be fancy on my part, and I persevered; but there was no mistaking it finally; and as she assured me she was not fatigued, which might have been some excuse, I had no choice but to attribute it to some unknown cause of offence on my part, or to some inexplicable caprice on hers."

"Or a little mixture of both," suggested his companion, laughing. "*Courage, mon ami!* let us beard the lion in his den, or in other words go and look for Miss de Burgh in the conservatory. I will accompany you, and help you to deliver your message; and I may perhaps arrive at some small conclusion on the subject. A woman's wits are generally sharper than a man's."

"Gratitude for your proffered service compels me to let that remark pass unheeded," replied Sir Charles, as he offered her his arm.

"You know my proposition is unanswerable," retorted Emily, saucily; "but that is a very neat way of getting out of your difficulty."

They crossed the broad *salon*, and traversed it to the further end, where it opened into a large and brilliantly-lighted conservatory.

Bending over a cluster of rare exotics stood Augusta. Count Salvi was by her side, and they were conversing in low tones; while impassioned glances from the dark eyes of the Italian rested on the beautiful English girl, though she saw them not, as her chief attention was apparently bestowed on the flowers she was so closely examining.

Such, however, was not the real state of the case. A chaos of dark passions filled the heart of Augusta. Had Count Salvi been able to read the expression of her downcast eyes, he had seen there no trace of any emotion that could have gratified him, unless in so far as it might have ministered to the evil qualities of his vengeful and crafty nature.

"Ah! there is Miss Crewe," the count had exclaimed, when that lady's voice was heard; "she is singing one of those eternal *ballades* of which she is so fond.   How inferior to those magnificent *scenas* to which you do such ample justice; they alone deserve the name of music."

Though she recognised the flattery, not particularly delicately administered, of this speech, it yet in some measure fell pleasantly on the ear of Augusta, who was, however, too proud to evince any gratification at the count's remark.

"Miss Crewe is a charming vocalist," she replied, with composure; "her voice is beautiful, and she has been well taught, besides having a strong natural taste.   One does not often hear a singer like her."

"Your opinion appears to be endorsed by Sir Charles Bellingham," observed Count Salvi maliciously; "he raves about *la belle Irlandaise* and her lovely voice everywhere. I left him paying her assiduous attention a few minutes ago; no doubt the *ballade* is the result of his supplication."

"If so, I am sure we are extremely indebted to him," replied Augusta, coldly, and what her companion felt to be bitterly.

"Without doubt," said Count Salvi, blandly; "it is a great pleasure to listen to the charming tones of Miss Crewe. Will you not advance nearer the doorway? You lose much of the effect at this distance; and you will enjoy it more if you both hear and see what is going on."

His words had a double meaning, as Augusta clearly perceived; but cowardice was foreign to her nature, and she chose to shrink from nothing that could enlighten her, however painful or humiliating to herself it might be.

She therefore stepped forward a few paces and stood at the entrance of the conservatory, where a full curtain of lace was looped up by marble pillars, and she could see well into the other room without being distinctly visible herself.

Count Salvi observed her manœuvre, but

he took no notice of it; he had obtained the object he desired, Miss de Burgh could now see and judge for herself—no comment of his was either necessary or advisable.

She saw the bright and beautiful Irish girl leaning gracefully on the antique *prie-dieu*—her head with its lustrous tresses thrown lightly back, her red lips softly parted as the rich tide of melody gushed from between them—and she saw Sir Charles Bellingham only a few paces distant, listening to her and gazing on her with an absorbed intentness that seemed to Augusta as though it could have only one meaning—an ardent attachment to the fair singer herself, so enthralling as to render him for the time blind and unconscious of all surrounding objects.

She contemplated this picture till the conclusion of the song, and then she turned calmly away and resumed her inspection of the flowers. But as she did so, the astute eye of the count noted the trembling of her hand when she occasionally touched an especially rare blossom, and he saw that she strove to conceal her countenance and avert her eyes. He therefore judged that her feelings were still keenly roused, only the force of an iron will had compelled them to assume the semblance of a composure she was yet far from experiencing in reality. Augusta felt grateful to Count Salvi for the quiet but assiduous attendance that for the time usurped that of others; and while not in the least intrusive, kept her thoughts in some measure off herself, and also compelled her in a slight degree to exert herself, which latter point she felt to be imperatively necessary.

So she yielded him a graceful and courteous, though perhaps a rather absent attention; and with this Count Salvi was for the present completely satisfied.

Presently voices were heard approaching the conservatory; it was Sir Charles Bellingham and Miss Crewe. We have already described their arrival and their errand.

Augusta recognised them, but she neither

moved nor spoke; only Count Salvi saw the slight clenching of the small white gloved hand, and heard the quickened respiration which alone betrayed the excitement under which she was labouring.

"Here is Miss de Burgh," exclaimed the gay voice of Emily Crewe. "Now, Sir Charles, you can make known your mission."

Augusta turned slowly round and faced them; but her expression was not particularly inviting, and Sir Charles felt some hesitation in delivering the message with which he had been entrusted.

"Lady A—— begged me to go in search of you, Miss de Burgh, and convey a request from her that you will be kind enough to oblige her guests and herself by singing something. She mentioned that she would await you at the piano if you are good enough to consent."

"I am sorry that I cannot oblige Lady A——," said Augusta, coldly. "It is very warm to-night, and I do not feel in good voice. I daresay she will have no difficulty in supplying my place."

"It were impossible!" exclaimed Count Salvi, enthusiastically ; "none can fill the place of Miss de Burgh."

Somewhat to the surprise both of Sir Charles Bellingham and Miss Crewe, Augusta bestowed a gracious look and sweet smile on the young Italian, as though gratified by the exaggerated fervour of his speech.

The count looked delighted, and was proceeding to utter a still warmer compliment, when Augusta interrupted him by again addressing Sir Charles. "Will you be kind enough to express my regret to Lady A——? Some other time I shall be happy to oblige her, but not this evening."

"Is your decision irrevocable?" said Sir Charles, who fancied he detected a lurking hesitation in her tone. "You inflict a severe disappointment on us all. I had been anticipating with much pleasure one of your beautiful Italian arias; for as Count Salvi truly observes, none can fill the place of Miss de Burgh."

"My decision is irrevocable," she replied, with a faint, dreary smile; "it is like the laws of the Medes and Persians. I cannot sing to-night."

"I fear Lady A—— will consider me a very feeble ambassador," said Sir Charles, courteously. "I hoped to have taken her a different reply. I am sorry you feel unequal to singing this evening."

He turned away with Miss Crewe, who had never quitted his arm, and re-entered the principal *salon*.

Augusta and the count were silent for a few minutes; the latter was rejoicing in the discomfiture of his supposed rival, while Augusta was meditating on all that had passed — at one moment half regretting her decision from a consideration of the motives to which it might not improbably be imputed; at the next, glad that she had remained firm, and proved to Count Salvi, Miss Crewe, and above all, to Sir Charles himself, that his wishes and requests were of little importance in her eyes.

While reflecting on this latter view of the

case a new line of action suggested itself to
her.

"Perhaps Lady A—— may think my
refusal rude," she suddenly remarked to
Count Salvi.

The crafty Italian partly guessed at her
motives, though he did not divine them
to their full extent. He saw, however,
that the triumph would lie with him could
Miss de Burgh now be prevailed on to re-
scind her determination; that the proposal
had not first emanated from him no one was
likely to discover.

"Fatigue and disinclination are an all-
sufficient apology," replied the count,
blandly; "but how delighted her ladyship will be should you announce that you
have changed your mind. It is a per-
mission accorded to all young ladies—one
of their peculiar privileges," he continued,
with a glittering smile. "Permit me to
add my humble supplications to those that
have gone before, and let me hope for a
more favourable result."

"I might perhaps sing a duet with you,"

said Augusta, after an instant of hesitation; "that is less of an exertion than singing alone."

"I shall be enchanted," replied the count, who felt that would indeed be a double triumph. "May I have the honour of conducting you to the piano, and of announcing your change of intention? Lady A—— can scarcely yet have quitted the place."

He offered his arm as he spoke, and Augusta accepted it. Something within her, that she could not analyse or restrain, kept urging her on to act as she was doing; so they left the conservatory, and followed in the direction already taken by Sir Charles Bellingham and Miss Crewe.

Scarcely had that couple entered the *salon*, and got beyond the hearing of those whom they had left behind, than Sir Charles remarked in an undertone to Emily, "You see, I was right. Her manner is quite dry and frigid."

"Undeniably so," replied Emily, laughing. "You are in Miss de Burgh's black books, *amico mio*."

"But I have done nothing to get into them," said Sir Charles, shrugging his shoulders. "That I am there is plain enough; but how did I get there?"

"How, indeed!" rejoined Emily, looking much amused. "We all know that young and beautiful ladies have their little caprices, Sir Charles. There is a little black dog at present reposing on the graceful shoulders of Miss de Burgh. Who put that little black dog there?"

"Not I, certainly," said the young man, laughing; "but I am very thickheaded, Miss Crewe, and never could understand parables or discover riddles. Nothing but good, plain, honest English will have any effect upon me."

"Oh! I must speak plainly, must I?" replied Emily, with a meaning smile. "Well, we shall see—not at present, however; for there is Lady A—— already looking disappointed that you are unaccompanied by the fair vocalist."

"Well, Sir Charles! Have you not been able to persuade Miss de Burgh to gratify

us?" inquired her ladyship. "I fancied
that in sending you I had selected a most
powerful ambassador, one whose demands
were not likely to be rejected!" Lady
A—— smiled and glanced archly at the
young baronet.

"I am very sorry that I have been an
unsuccessful envoy," replied Sir Charles,
all unconscious of the double meaning contained in her remark. "Miss de Burgh
was not to be prevailed on to give her consent. She pleaded heat and inability to
sing: the truth is she took a long drive
to-day, and, though she denies having felt
fatigue in consequence, I am persuaded it
was too much for her. At all events I did
my utmost, and the result is a mortifying
failure."

"Then I must be doubly proud of my success," sounded clearly and distinctly behind
them; and as all turned hastily round, for
they were grouped round the piano, having
their backs towards the conservatory, Count
Salvi and Miss de Burgh stood beside
them, an expression of crafty triumph

shining in the dark eyes of the Italian, and perceptible even in the melodious tones of his soft liquid voice. " I am quite proud of having induced Miss de Burgh to alter her resolution of not singing this evening," continued the count, as he made way for Augusta to approach the instrument; " I hardly thought to succeed where others had failed."

This was not quite true, and Augusta knew it was not: but it suited her that the count's version should be believed, and Sir Charles Bellingham have the mortification of perceiving that Count Salvi's petition had been granted while his had been refused.

She seated herself at the piano, and ran her fingers over the keys in a light and brilliant prelude. Then she sang with the count one of those exquisite duets which so admirably displayed their two perfect voices. Never had she sung more splendidly; the room was hushed in an instant, as if by magic; while to its farthest corner rolled the full tide of rich harmony, and even the lingerers in distant corridors were arrested

by the thrilling tones of the two matchless
'vocalists.

A torrent of applause greeted the close
of the performance; and Miss de Burgh
was surrounded by eager admirers, who
warmly expressed their gratitude to the
count and herself for the great treat they
had afforded them.

But one usually approving voice was
silent: there was no word of comment or
gratification from Sir Charles Bellingham,
and Augusta felt that she missed it.

He had listened with calm attention to
the music; but on its conclusion he made
no attempt to join the group round the
piano: and when Miss de Burgh was
sufficiently at liberty to observe what was
going on in her neighbourhood, Sir Charles
was once more in earnest conversation with
Emily Crewe.

The remainder of the evening was a blank
to Augusta; and when at length it came to
an end, she saw with heartfelt satisfaction
the gradual dispersion of the company, and
was thankful to observe her father coming

towards her with, as she truly guessed, the welcome announcement of their carriage having arrived. She rose at once, and bowing a graceful adieu to her *entourage*, she accepted the arm of Count Salvi, who stood beside her, ever watchful and ready.

As they went to take leave of Lord and Lady A——, they passed the sofa where Sir Charles Bellingham still sat conversing with Miss Crewe. He looked up accidentally as they passed, and a grave and formal salutation took place between Augusta and himself.

"How very dignified and proper we have become all of a sudden," said Emily, laughing, when Count Salvi and his fair companion were out of hearing. "You will have some little difficulty in getting out of those black books, Sir Charles."

"The cause of my disgrace is still an enigma," replied the young baronet; "which reminds me, Miss Crewe, that you promised me the assistance of your keen 'woman's wit,' and also an explanation in language suited to my dull capacity. Behold the time, the place, and the man."

"I did not promise," replied the young lady; "I only said I should see about it."

"That is quite equal to a promise," retorted Sir Charles; "and I am so eager for information that it would be cruel not to enlighten my ignorance."

"When I was young," said Miss Crewe, with affected gravity, "the denser brains among juveniles were generally instructed by means of short and simple stories adapted to each particular capacity. Perhaps that style may suit you best?"

"Not a doubt on the subject," replied Sir Charles, laughing; "my brains are frightfully thick; a story is the only thing likely to make an impression on them."

"I like fairy stories best," said Emily, "therefore it shall be a fairy tale. Well— once on a time—they all begin in that way, you know."

"Of course they do," replied her companion. "Go on, Miss Crewe—I am getting quite excited—once on a time——"

"Once on a time, Sir Charles, there was

a king's son; and he had, as was customary
then with kings' sons, a fairy godmother."

"Dear old lady! — fortunate young
man!" interjected Sir Charles.

"Now, if you interrupt me, I won't say
another word."

"A thousand pardons, my dear Miss
Crewe; but the good luck of that king's
son excited a momentary feeling of envy."

"A fairy godmother was not always a
blessing," continued Emily; "they were
very spiteful sometimes, and did fully more
mischief than good. However, in this particular instance, the old lady had been properly treated; and being politely invited to
the christening of the prince, she accepted
the invitation, and appeared there in the
most amiable humour possible, in high
satisfaction with all the royal family, and
especially delighted with her young godson.
She showered fairy gifts on the little
prince: she made him good, brave, handsome, rich, amiable, and fascinating—in
short, a regular paragon!" Miss Crewe
laughed softly to herself, and pausing for

a moment, she contemplated the young baronet through her half-closed eyes, in which an expression of wicked merriment was distinctly visible.

"What a very charming young man," replied Sir Charles, returning her glance; "I wish fairy godmothers had been in fashion in my infancy."

"All these gifts she bestowed upon him," continued Miss Crewe; "and last of all she produced a rich silk and gold handkerchief, all covered with precious stones and embroidery. This, she declared, was her crowning gift; for when the young prince should be grown up, every person to whom he handed it would be perfectly charmed with him, and take the greatest delight in his society. It did not matter who it was, for the time they must all succumb to the power of this magic handkerchief: and when the young prince became a man, he found that this was really the case, and that the old lady had not exaggerated its magic influence in the very least.

"He discovered that the possession of the

handkerchief was very useful, and also at times extremely amusing. At his father's royal court were a number of very pretty young ladies, and to each of those he used to hand the handkerchief in turn———"

"Really, Miss Crewe!" exclaimed Sir Charles, half rising, and looking at the same time slightly annoyed.

"What is the matter?" inquired Emily, with an air of perfect candour and innocence.

"Nothing," replied Sir Charles, trying to look equally unconscious; "I am afraid this king's son was a very naughty young prince. He seems to have been a sad flirt."

"So the courtiers all said," observed Miss Crewe; "but he was only amusing himself all the time, and he meant not the slightest harm. When he gave the handkerchief to a young lady, she curtseyed and took it; and when she had held it long enough, and he had had a very pleasant conversation with her, he requested her to return it to him; and she curtseyed again, and immediately gave it him back."

"What a very charming arrangement," said Sir Charles, laughing; "really, Miss Crewe, this fairy tale of yours is extremely interesting."

"But you must hear the end of it," continued Emily, holding up a warning forefinger. "It happened sometimes that the young ladies admired the handkerchief so much, and grew so fond of the fascinating prince, that when he had had enough of them, and wished back the handkerchief, they were not always quite willing to return it. Still, in the end they generally did give it him back."

"Poor little things! it was very hard on them," said Sir Charles. "Now, I should have been wiser than that king's son, Miss Crewe. I would have torn the handkerchief into little bits, and given each of them a morsel, first reserving one large portion for future contingencies."

"Strangely enough, Sir Charles, the same idea has suggested itself to you that occurred to the prince. But, unfortunately, fairy gifts had always a condition attached

to them; and when the young prince attempted the destruction of his handkerchief,
he was immediately informed by some mysterious agency that very dreadful calamities
would follow his persistence in such a course.
So he had no resource but to submit to his
fate, and this wonderful fascination of his
rather increased than diminished. But
hitherto nothing very serious had befallen
him; he led the pleasantest life possible, and
most people thought he was a young prince
exceedingly to be envied."

"Exactly my opinion," said Sir Charles.

"But at last there came to the court of
the king, his father, the most beautiful
young lady that ever was seen. All her
life long everybody had adored her; and she
had become so accustomed to this worship
that she took it quite as a matter of course,
and never dreamt of being expected to do
anything that was in the least disagreeable
to her."

"Very badly trained she must have been,
Miss Crewe."

"No doubt," replied Emily; "but that

was not exactly her fault, poor thing! Well, she was so beautiful, and so charming in every way, that no sooner did the young prince see her than he fell in love with her that very minute; and, immediately producing his magnificent handkerchief, he made her a very polite bow, and requested her to honour him by taking it into her lily hand."

"Oh! Miss Crewe! Miss Crewe!" said Sir Charles, shaking his head reproachfully.

"Are you weary of my story?" asked Emily, smiling; "it is very nearly done now."

"Oh! I must hear the end of it," he replied, laughing.

"Well, the prince was so delighted with this charming young lady, that for a long time he never thought about his handkerchief; and when at last he wished it returned and asked her for it, she was quite amazed and very indignant, having entirely forgotten or else not understood that he had only lent it to her. Look, Sir Charles, there is Norah making signs to me, and the room is getting very empty; we must be going now."

"But you have not finished your story yet," urged her companion; "I must know if the prince got back his handkerchief. Why, that is the very point of the tale."

"Exactly," replied Emily, rising, and glancing at him, with a meaning smile; "but that is just what I can't tell you. The pages were very stupidly torn at that part, and I don't know whether the beautiful young lady was at last brought to hear reason or not.   But the tale was a kind of allegory, you know; and the application fortunately had not been torn out——"

"Oh! spare me the application," said Sir Charles, hurriedly offering her his arm; looking at the same time rather confused, which he attempted to cover with a laugh. "I am far too stupid to understand anything of the kind.   The tale is charming; pray don't spoil it by deducing morals and trite observations.   When I read fairy legends in my juvenile days, I always made a point of skipping the application."

"Good advice is sometimes useful, Sir Charles," replied Miss Crewe, with a smile; "and the application of that tale was rather a sensible one."

"I have not a doubt of it," said the young baronet, as he led her to join her sister; "perhaps I shall try to puzzle it out at home. Thank you all the same for your delightful story; you have quite a gift in that line, Miss Crewe."

CHAPTER III.

ONE of the last balls of the season was to come off the next night at the palazzo of the Duca di R——, and it was also expected to prove one of the very best and most brilliant. Every one was going, at least all the *crême de la crême* of the society in Rome; and the two reigning beauties had of course been requested to grace the ball with their presence. It so happened that among the list of music selected for the occasion was a new and favourite waltz, called the "Valse d'Egérie." It was the composition of a French musician residing in Rome; who having received several important services from Sir John de Burgh, had striven in some measure to show his gratitude by dedicating the really graceful piece of music to his daughter.

The waltz was an especial favourite with Augusta, and also with Sir Charles Bellingham; and it had gradually come to be an almost established custom that whenever it chanced to be played they danced it together; no distinct understanding existed on the subject, nevertheless they always did it.

That evening, for a whim, Augusta was dressed in black. The superb diamonds of the De Burgh family had long ago been reset and presented to her by her father, who grudged nothing that could adorn or gratify his favourite daughter. A coronet of dazzling stars graced her fair brow, and many ornaments of the same costly gems glittered on her bosom and her white rounded arms. She looked more like a brilliant young matron than an unmarried girl, as her father led her into the Duke's stately reception-room, where all that was distinguished and attractive in the society of the Roman capital had that night assembled at the bidding of the noble host.

"Here is a seat, Miss de Burgh," said a

cordial voice just behind them as they walked up the room; and on turning round, Augusta perceived Lady Agnes Bellingham making room for her on a sofa. It looked ungracious to refuse the friendly offer; Augusta had no excuse ready, so she quitted her father's arm and took a seat by the side of Lady Agnes.

Sir John de Burgh entered into conversation with the old lady; and while they were so engaged Augusta glanced round the crowded apartment. Almost immediately she perceived Sir Charles Bellingham; he was conversing with a gentleman at some little distance, but he chanced to look up at the moment, and their eyes met. Taken by surprise, Augusta bowed hastily, and felt that she coloured as she did so: she was much annoyed at her want of presence of mind, more especially as Sir Charles returned her bow gravely, and after a few minutes' further conversation with his friend he quitted the place where they had been standing, and entered the adjoining ball-room.

With a blank feeling at her heart which she scorned to admit even to herself, Augusta strove to address some remarks to the unconscious Lady Agnes. While she was doing so, the music, which had been silent for a short interval, recommenced; a few familiar chords broke on her ear, and then the flowing melody of the "Valse d'Egérie" summoned the dancers to resume the amusement of the evening.

Augusta instantly recognised her favourite; she wondered if Sir Charles did so also, and if according to long-established custom, he would claim her as his partner for the dance.

" I am engaged," was her reply to a young Austrian baron who begged for the honour of her hand: the baron bowed and withdrew.

Several other would-be partners received the same answer: the waltz had barely commenced, and Augusta felt reluctant to deprive herself of the chance of dancing it with Sir Charles.

" What a pity that your partner does not come, my dear," said Lady Agnes, kindly; " perhaps he may not think of looking for you here.   Had you not better accept some one else? You can explain it to him afterwards."

"It does not matter," said Augusta, in a tone of indifference; "I am rather glad of an excuse for sitting still."

But Lady Agnes was not unobservant, and she had noticed a frown flit across the countenance of her fair companion as the gay strains of the waltz continued, and still the recusant partner came not.

"Who can it be?" mused the old lady: "not Charles, certainly — he was here a short time ago, and must have seen her. Perhaps it is Count Salvi."

The count was near at that moment, nearer than either she or Miss de Burgh imagined; he had watched Augusta ever since she had entered the room, and he had thoroughly penetrated her behaviour and the motives that led to it.

"She is waiting for Sir Charles," he muttered to himself, and a lowering scowl contracted his forehead.   "What fools women are! Can she not see that the cold

Englishman has no thought of her?—values her only as the pleasant companion of an idle hour! While I!—I would die for her!—die for those smiles she lavishes so freely on him, and which he scarcely heeds!"

But no Sir Charles appeared, and Count Salvi's meditations took a different turn. With his crafty Italian nature and imagination, he allowed no chance to escape him.

He saw Miss de Burgh reject partner after partner, and arrived at the conclusion either that she was not dancing from choice, or that her negligent partner was Sir Charles Bellingham, and that he had forgotten the engagement. A moment's reflection decided his line of conduct.

He advanced quickly to the door leading into the ball-room, and saw, as he expected, Sir Charles Bellingham engaged in dancing: he saw also that his partner was Miss Crewe, a stroke of good fortune he had scarcely dared to anticipate, and which he instantly resolved to turn still further to his own advantage.

Directing his steps to the place where Lady Agnes and Augusta were sitting, he affected to perceive them then for the first time.

"Ah! Miss de Burgh," he exclaimed, joyfully, "I have been looking for you everywhere. How have you chosen so secluded a seat? May I not hope to finish this charming waltz with you? It will last for some time yet."

Augusta hesitated for a moment, and then she rose and took his arm.

"It is too late to join this dance I think," she replied; "but I will take a turn in the vestibule, it is very warm here."

"It was not Count Salvi," said Lady Agnes to herself, as the young couple retreated towards the doorway; "surely it was not Charles after all; I must ask him."

The count and Augusta passed slowly along the vestibule.

"Were you engaged for this dance?" inquired Count Salvi: "will you not finish it with me?"

"I was engaged," replied Miss de Burgh,

calmly, "but my partner did not appear. I suppose he could not find me, or had forgotten his engagement."

"Surely that were impossible!" said the count, eagerly. "Could any one forget such an engagement as that? If so, his feelings must indeed be unenviably frigid. Had I been so pledged, it had obliterated all else from my memory."

"My partner is less devoted, it seems," replied Augusta, striving to answer him lightly, for he was disposed to be too complimentary for her taste.

"He could not be more so," said the count, in a low and impassioned tone, while he bent forward and tried to read the expression of her carefully averted eyes.

Augusta felt uncomfortable, for two or three people glanced curiously at them as they passed. The vestibule opened on a low marble terrace that nearly surrounded the house, and communicated with the garden by flights of stone steps placed at intervals along it.

The wide entrance door stood invitingly

open, and the bright beams of the glorious southern moon bathed terrace and garden in their pure silvery radiance.

"How lovely!" exclaimed the count, as they paused for an instant to contemplate the beauty of the scene. "A stroll round the terrace would be charming. Will you come?"

He drew her gently forward as he spoke, and Augusta yielded to the slight coercion he employed; they strolled on for a few minutes in silence, while through the widely-opened windows came the soft notes of the "Valse d'Egérie," and Augusta listened to them as they rose and fell, with many bitter thoughts in her mind.

"It is indeed most exquisite," she remarked, as they paused in their walk to watch the brilliant effect produced by the moonbeams falling on the light spray of a fountain. "How charmingly the gardens here are laid out!—so much variety."

"Astonishing!" replied the count, in rather an absent tone. A dissertation on landscape gardening did not exactly suit the present state of his feelings. He glanced anxiously round. No one was near, but a window opened on the terrace not half a dozen yards from where they stood; and as Augusta remained in apparently fixed contemplation of the fountain, the count stole from her side for a moment, and advancing on tiptoe to the window, he gazed cautiously into the room beyond. What he saw there caused his heart to throb with irrepressible exultation, and forced a sudden exclamation from his lips.

Augusta looked round as he did so, and observed his eager gaze.

" What is it?" she inquired, with a careless smile. " What do you see that is so interesting ? "

" Look here," replied Count Salvi, after an instant of hesitation. " I think you will allow that it is interesting—to you, at least;" and he glanced at her with a questioning and sinister expression.

Miss de Burgh languidly approached the window; Count Salvi watched her with breathless anxiety as she reached it and looked into the room. In an instant her air of stately indifference was gone: she started back as though she had been stung, and an expression flashed from her dark eyes before which Count Salvi, all exultant the previous moment, quailed and fell back abashed and humiliated.

In that room sat Sir Charles Bellingham and Miss Crewe: so completely engrossed with each other and with their occupation, that neither of them observed the two dark forms that had so earnestly regarded them. Miss Crewe was explaining to Sir Charles the proper manner of using a fan; and at the instant in which Augusta caught sight of them the young lady was laughingly repossessing herself of her fan, which Sir Charles was awkwardly unfurling; and her peal of silvery laughter was blended with the last softly dying notes of the " Valse d'Egérie," which the orchestra in the adjacent ball-room was just ceasing to perform.

It was a moment of intense bitterness to Augusta; and though in proud disdain she retreated from the window, scorning the position of spy that had been so unwittingly forced upon her, she could not so rapidly still the agonized beating of her heart, or command the voice in which she would fain have desired Count Salvi to quit her presence on the instant.

For all his motives lay bare before her; and a strong hatred entered into her soul against the man who could so cruelly and ungenerously seek her trial and humiliation. The count saw that he had gone too far; the haughty pride and indignation written on her countenance told him that: and so far as lay in his power he endeavoured to retrieve his error.

"Miss de Burgh! Augusta!" he whispered, bending low on the ground before her; "forgive me—hear me but for a moment?"

"Silence, sir!" she replied, in the same tone; "would you have them know that we are here—acting as spies on them in the darkness of the night?"

He seized the small hand that hung by

her side, and forcibly withdrew her some paces from the window.

"Leave me!" said Augusta, resolutely, as she strove to release herself from his grasp. "I wish to hear nothing that you can say to me. You think you have mortified and annoyed me—your task is completed, and I trust you are satisfied. Leave me now; I wish to be alone."

"I will not go till you have heard me—then, if you still wish it, I will leave you."

"Have your will, then," replied Augusta, with cutting disdain; "but I beg you will inflict on me as few words as possible. I am in no mood to listen to you, believe me, Count Salvi."

"And yet I love you, Augusta—so dearly —so dearly!" urged the count, passionately. "Surely you must have seen it—known it." He gazed at her with a melancholy earnestness that might have touched her at another time; but now her heart was steeled against his entreaties, and she hated him only the more bitterly for his misplaced attachment. She did not reply, and he continued in a sadder tone—

"Till lately I had dared to hope, presumptuous as it may appear to you;" for Augusta had made a haughty gesture of dissent. "We had been much together—I had ever been received with favour, nay, even treated with a blissful distinction. I had drunk in the music of your voice, basked in the sunshine of your smiles, gazed on your glorious beauty till I could resist it no longer, and I yielded to a passion unknown among the men of your cold northern clime. With them it is a tranquil, measured feeling, which they can apparently indulge or restrain at pleasure—with us it is as a raging torrent, breaking down every barrier, defying all efforts to hold it in tame subjection."

"It has certainly broken down a good many barriers in your case," said Augusta, with icy coldness, "when it has led you to transgress the commonest rules of ordinary courtesy and gentlemanly feeling."

Count Salvi started, and drew himself up to his full height.

"You may taunt me if you will," he replied, haughtily; "but even if it is unwelcome to you, love such as mine merits respect and not scorn. For months past my heart has beat only for you, Augusta; its every pulse has throbbed and quickened at your approach. Can you say as much for yon phlegmatic Englishman, to whom you have given the love that I would yield worlds to obtain—who values your preference so little, that while you were fruitlessly waiting for him to claim your hand in the dance, he was toying and jesting with the red-haired Irish rival, who usurps even more of his notice than you do yourself?"

Augusta writhed beneath the withering sarcasm, which proved how entirely the count was acquainted with all that related to the events of the evening; but her will, when she chose, was of iron determination, and by no word or look would she betray the misery that Count Salvi's humiliating accusation caused her, though the torture

she was enduring blanched her countenance
to a pallor like death, and her trembling
limbs felt as though they could hardly sus-
tain her exhausted form.

"Who is using taunts now?" she said,
still in the same cold thrilling tone. "Have
you nearly finished your courteous observations, Count Salvi? Because, if so, perhaps
you will be good enough to leave me, as
you promised to do."

The count uttered an exclamation of
bitter irritation, and extended his hands in
an appealing manner.

"Not a word—not one single word, in
return for all this love that I have lavished
on you! Are you, indeed, so little of a
woman? I have heard them say that you
have no heart—but surely you cannot disdain love such as mine! A queen might
be proud to know that a heart existed
which throbbed only for her!"

"Very possibly," replied Augusta, in
an indifferent manner; "but, not being a
queen, I value your pretended love as it
deserves; a selfish passion, aiming only at

its own gratification, with no scruple as to inflicting pain or humiliation on the object it yet affects to idolize."

Count Salvi clenched his hands passionately. "Heartless! heartless!" he exclaimed, bitterly; "but will you forgive me if I sue in the dust for pardon; if I own that in the blind frenzy of my love I acted rashly—unkindly, if you will? I thought it might make you think differently if you saw how lightly your preference was esteemed by him on whom you had bestowed it; while——"

"You dare to insult me again, Count Salvi!" said Augusta, proudly interrupting him. "Silence! and listen to me now. Your love is valueless in my eyes; worse than valueless, I regard it as an insult from a man such as you have proved yourself to be. Till to-night I have at least looked on you as a gentleman: now I do so no longer. But if you have the slightest self-respect left, if you would ever regain the position in my eyes that this evening's work has forfeited, be silent on what has occurred.

But I exact no promise from you; I do not even ask it as a favour; I leave it entirely to yourself. And now be so good as to allow me to pass."

She drew her draperies around her as if to avoid touching him, and turned towards a flight of steps that led into the garden.

"One single word before you go, Miss de Burgh," said Count Salvi with a haughtiness equal to her own. "You have despised me, but it may not always be so. The events of this evening shall never pass from my memory, but they shall equally never cross my lips. Farewell!"

The next instant he passed rapidly along the terrace, and turning the corner of the palace was lost to sight.

Miss de Burgh paused for a few moments irresolutely, and then she slowly descended the steps into the garden, and disappeared down one of its dark alleys.

CHAPTER IV.

TURNING THE TABLES.

HAD Augusta looked for only another moment on the tableau presented to her by the jealous intervention of Count Salvi, she would have perceived an immediate change in the position of the two persons who composed it.

For the softly dying notes of the " Valse d'Egérie" fell on other ears than those of the pale watcher on the terrace ; the familiar chords struck home to the remembrance of Sir Charles Bellingham, and an exclamation of surprise and vexation escaped his lips.

" What's the matter?" inquired Miss Crewe, suspending operations on her fan ; " have you seen a ghost?"

" The ghost of an unfulfilled engagement

has risen to reproach me," replied Sir Charles, rather ruefully. "Miss Crewe, you have much to answer for: it is all your fault."

"Ah! you ought to have been dancing with some one else instead of wasting your time here with me, and you expect me to help you out of your dilemma. Who is the offended fair one?"

"I believe I should have danced this waltz with Miss de Burgh," replied Sir Charles, with some slight hesitation.

"Miss de Burgh!" said Miss Crewe, looking at him with steady composure; "you will not find it quite so easy to lay that ghost, and I fear I shall rather hinder than help. You must make your own peace in that quarter, Sir Charles."

"I suppose I must," he replied, rather avoiding her glance. "The waltz is over now, so reparation is impossible."

"Repentance only remains," observed Emily, with decorous gravity, rather disturbed by a slight twinkle in her eye. "Get me a seat somewhere, and then cast

about in your mind for a handsome apology.
A proper fit of penitence, and I think you
may hope for forgiveness."

They quitted the apartment in which they
had been sitting, and Miss Crewe found a
seat beside some friends. Sir Charles went
instantly to the spot where he had formerly
seen Augusta; but, as we are aware, she
was no longer to be found there. Lady
Agnes still retained her seat, however, and
to her Sir Charles applied for information.

" Do you know what has become of Miss
de Burgh?" he inquired; " I left her sitting
beside you."

" Oh! Charles, were you the partner for
whom she waited so long?" said Lady Agnes,
reproachfully. " Why were you so negligent
as not to remember your engagement?"

" Do you know, my dear mother, that
yours is rather a Scotch answer?" observed
her son, with a smile. "I am sure I am
exceedingly distressed that I kept Miss de
Burgh waiting for me; but she has not
exactly waited, for she is not here now."

" She did wait, however, till the dance

was nearly finished," said Lady Agnes; "and I am sure she did not like it: one can generally discover when Miss de Burgh is displeased," continued the old lady, seriously.

" That is an unquestionable fact," replied the young baronet, laughing; "Miss de Burgh does not always disguise her sentiments. All the more reason for my apologizing to her now when I am decidedly in fault. Where has she gone to?"

" That I cannot tell you," said his mother; " Count Salvi wished her to waltz with him, but she declined him, as she had done several others; till I began to fear it was for you that she was waiting. But she went away with the count at last, to walk in the vestibule I think she said."

A shade of annoyance passed over the countenance of the young baronet.

" That eternal fellow Salvi!" he muttered to himself. " I hate his very name. Well, I suppose I must find her and make an apology for my tardiness," he added aloud. " Should she return here, mother, you may mention that I am in the depths of despair, and have gone off in search of her to express my contrition."

Lady Agnes smiled, and her eyes followed her son as he crossed the apartment, and finally passed into the vestibule, and towards the open window, through which the count and Augusta had quitted it scarcely half an hour before. The glorious moonlight that had attracted them, excited his admiration also: and yielding to the seductive influence of the scene before him, he too stepped out a few paces on the terrace, and silently gazed on the deep blue starlit sky, where the queen of night floated softly among light masses of fleecy clouds, now casting the garden and its turfen walks into dim shadow, and the next instant bathing it in a flood of silvery sheen, beneath which each tiny dewdrop glistened and twinkled as though diamond dust had been profusely scattered on every bush and parterre.

Sir Charles slowly descended the flight of steps that led to the garden immediately beneath; and as if the same spirit guided

him that had so lately guided a fairer wanderer, he turned down the very same path
by which Augusta had sought the darkest
seclusion and solitude of the garden.

Insensibly his thoughts reverted to Miss
de Burgh and her strange behaviour; her
unmistakeable coldness and even hauteur at
one time, and her no less undisguised preference at another. He began to think that
after all he could scarcely have been expected to consider himself bound to her for
the waltz, when all the circumstances of her
recent treatment of him were taken into
account.

It had certainly been their custom to
dance that particular waltz together, but
the engagement had been merely an implied
one; no regular understanding had existed
on the subject.

Therefore, reviewing the case calmly
and dispassionately, Sir Charles was just
arriving at the conclusion that he had been
disturbing himself very unnecessarily, and
that he was in reality the injured party, and
not Miss de Burgh at all, when his medita-

tions were suddenly cut short by a low suppressed cry which sounded as though uttered in his immediate vicinity. The turf on which he walked deadened all noise of footsteps, and the humming of the "Valse d'Egérie" had ceased for several minutes, so there was nothing to warn any persons who might be in the neighbourhood that they were not alone in their seclusion. Sir Charles stopped instantly, and listened for a repetition of the cry. He had not long to wait. It was repeated again and again, each time with increasing bitterness; and low choked murmurs in what seemed to be a woman's voice, interrupted by the sound of convulsive weeping, fell distinctly on his ear.

"Good heavens! who can it be?" he muttered to himself, as he softly approached the spot where the mourner was evidently concealed. It was a small clump of evergreens planted thickly together; and the place was entirely shaded by the branches of a large tree, no moonbeam being able to penetrate the dense masses of foliage.

Still there was light sufficient to enable Sir Charles to distinguish a dark form huddled together on the ground, as if it had fallen there or thrown itself down in an extremity of anguish. The flowing garments were those of a woman; and the young baronet was about to stoop forward and whisper some words of kind inquiry and sympathy, when a white arm was thrown violently upwards, the diamonds that encircled it glittering brightly in the moonlight, and an exclamation was uttered in a voice he knew only too well, and which transfixed him in silent horror and amazement in the very spot and attitude in which he heard it.

"Fool that I am! wretched, miserable fool!" murmured in broken accents the voice of Augusta de Burgh, as she lay there in an abandonment of grief and despair; "to dream that he cared for me, or ever gave one moment's thought to me! But it is all over now—for ever—for ever!" A fresh burst of weeping succeeded, and Sir Charles began to feel his position most awkward,

and to long to escape from it unperceived.
He never doubted that Count Salvi was the
person to whom Miss de Burgh alluded;
and he felt how terribly annoyed she would
be if she made the unwelcome discovery
that another was in possession of so mortifying a revelation.

"Poor girl!" he mentally ejaculated,
"who would have given her credit for
feelings like this, with that calm stately
manner? I really wish I could say something to comfort her; but the thing is
impossible—I only wish I were well out of
this. What a brute the fellow must be;
what can he have been saying or doing to
her? I wonder if I should speak to her or
not: it seems cruel to leave her here in
this state."

While he hesitated Augusta spoke once
more.

"He cared for me once—yes, I am sure
he loved me once—till she came with her
hateful smile and honeyed words, and lured
him from me. I could have killed her as
she sat with him in that room to-night,

keeping him there when I was waiting for him—waiting for one who did not even remember my existence!" The jewelled hand fell heavily on the turf, and the queenly head with its wealth of glorious tresses sunk yet lower in utter misery and self-abasement.

As though from the bite of a scorpion Sir Charles Bellingham started violently; and a cold dew of horror stood thick and clammy on his brow.

What did those words mean?

What horrible mystery lay before him?

Of whom was Miss de Burgh now speaking—surely not of himself?

Not a moment remained to him for retreat or reflection. His half-uttered ejaculation of amazement caused Augusta to look hastily up; as she did so the moonbeams illuminated her pale features, on which was stamped an expression half of terror, half of menace.

"Why are you here? whom are you seeking?" she asked, boldly confronting him; though her slight form writhed and shivered with shame and agony, and it was with difficulty she forced the words from between her pallid lips. "Can you not speak? What have you heard?" she continued, wildly; for through pure inability to answer her Sir Charles had remained silent. "Are you too here to taunt me with my folly and its consequences?"

"Far from it," he replied, in accents of the deepest pity; "my presence in this spot is the merest accident; and if I have learnt anything of which before I was ignorant, surely you know me better, Miss de Burgh, than to think that I should feel otherwise than proud of an implied preference only too flattering to my poor deserts."

"Pshaw!" she exclaimed, with a gesture of contemptuous disdain; "I know what that means: but you cannot despise me more thoroughly than I despise myself. Be very sure of that. I know how men think of a woman who forgets the dignity of her sex and bestows her love unsought: but you are a gentleman, Sir Charles, and my miserable secret is safe with you.

Forget, if you can, that you have ever heard it."

She had risen from the ground as she spoke, and now stood by his side under the deep shade of the evergreens.

Sir Charles Bellingham took her reluctant hand in his, and looked at her gravely for a moment. Her eyes were carefully averted from him, so he could not read their expression; but he felt the convulsive trembling of her fingers, and in that moment of silence and mutual embarrassment his determined resolve was taken. He would ask Augusta de Burgh to be his wife.

"I do not wish to forget what I have heard, Miss de Burgh," he replied, earnestly; "unless it is your express desire that I should do so. Will you permit me to speak to you for a few moments? I shall not detain you long."

She inclined her head gravely in reply, and Sir Charles continued.

"We have been acquaintances, I think I may venture to say friends, for some months now, Miss de Burgh; and though

I trust I am not what is called a vain man, yet I will dare to hope that you have formed a favourable opinion of me in so far at least as regards my principles and my honourable feelings. Will you do me justice so far as to allow this?"

"Certainly," replied Augusta, gently. "I have every confidence in you, Sir Charles."

"Then," he added, still retaining her hand in a firm pressure, "let me say a few words more to you, and hear me patiently to the end. When I came here this evening, I mean into the garden, nothing was farther from my thoughts than the prospect of finding you here. It was an entirely accidental *rencontre;* and had I been aware of the circumstances of the case, I should most decidedly have avoided a meeting calculated to distress you and wound your feelings."

With an exclamation as of one in pain Augusta turned away her head, and strove to withdraw her hand.

"Nay, but you must hear me," said Sir Charles, clasping it still more tightly; "I should without doubt have acted in this manner: now I am only too glad it has happened otherwise. So little was I aware of the state of your feelings towards me, and of the flattering preference of which I am the unworthy object, that when in the stillness of the night I heard a sudden cry as of pain, and listening recognised your voice, I imagined the expressions of which I became the unwilling auditor, referred not to myself, but to Count Salvi."

"To Count Salvi!" exclaimed Augusta, interrupting him indignantly; "he is the object of my scorn and loathing!"

"That feeling must surely have been very recently inspired by him," said Sir Charles, quietly. "Until this evening you have apparently been on the very best of terms; and I heard of your being seen with him scarcely an hour ago. Nay, Miss de Burgh, if you will have it, your own conduct quite lately seemed naturally enough to point him out as especially favoured by you. How long is it since you refused to sing at my request, and yielded immediately to his? Your behaviour on that occasion hurt me deeply, I do not pretend to deny it; for we had always been very good friends, and so far as I was aware I had done nothing to merit your displeasure."

"Must I confess the miserable truth?" replied Augusta, covering her face with her disengaged hand. "It was acting, all acting; a flimsy veil by which I hoped to screen my weakness, and hide my humiliating secret from public gaze. But he saw through it—he told me he had known it all along—and there were times when he was able to turn it to his own advantage, and induce me to play out the false part I had assigned to myself. That night when I sung at his request was one of them. Now, am I sufficiently degraded in your eyes? Do you despise me too much to pity me? Miserable fool that I am!" and she again strove to release herself from his grasp.

"Augusta!" exclaimed Sir Charles, with sudden and strong passion, "do not distress yourself any more by expressions such as these, so utterly the opposite of every sentiment I have ever felt towards you!

The vainest of men could not be otherwise than flattered by finding himself regarded with preference by such a woman as you! Let me hear from your own lips that you will continue that preference—that if I do possess your heart, I may now sue for the possession of your hand. And let me add, that though I am not a man given to much profession or demonstration, I will yet venture to affirm that I shall prize your love as my most cherished treasure, and that you shall never have cause to rue the day when a fortunate chance revealed to me a secret which but for that accident might· never have become known to me."

He spoke with much warmth and eagerness; and when he had finished, he tried with his other hand to draw her yet closer to him that he might read her answer in her downcast countenance; but Augusta silently and gravely repelled him.

"It is kindly meant," she said at length, struggling with her deep emotion; "your words are kind and generous as the heart that inspired them. But oh! Sir Charles, I am indeed sunk and fallen in your eyes when you can dream that I would accept a proposal like this—that because you are good and noble enough to be willing to sacrifice yourself for me, you believe that I would be the degraded creature to accept that sacrifice. No! no! Sir Charles! It may be that an error like mine deserves a severe punishment; but that you should judge of me like this is very bitter, very hard to bear!"

"Augusta!" replied Sir Charles, still more eagerly, "you misjudge both yourself and me. It is not from motives of pity or compassion that I speak as I have now done: do not imagine this for a moment. I admire you more than any woman I have ever seen—I have always admired you—but I have always too felt my admiration repelled by what seemed to me your indifference and coldness. There were times when I appeared to hold a higher position in your eyes—but it has not been so for a long time past: I confess that I had attributed the change to the influence of Count Salvi, and felt that he had gained that place in your regard which I would have given worlds to obtain. Now that I am aware how false was this impression — now that I have learnt from your own sweet lips that you love me, all unworthy as I am—let me add that it needed only the encouragement I now feel to urge me to a confession which you should have heard long ago, had I thought it would have met with a moment's favour in your eyes."

"Sir Charles! Sir Charles!" said Augusta, trying, though more faintly, to disengage herself from his grasp; "you are deceiving me, and you know you are. You have no real love for me; nay, more, you tell me that you imagined my preference was for Count Salvi—I, on my part, was equally convinced that your love was given to Miss Crewe. Can you look me in the face and deny this?"

"I can indeed, and I do;" replied the young baronet, bending over the lovely blushing countenance he strove to raise to his own. "Should I be speaking to you like this were Miss Crewe anything more to me than a friend—a valued friend, I allow—but one for whom I have never entertained a warmer sentiment?"

Truth compels us to own, however, that as Sir Charles uttered these words, a vision of the fair Emily flitted across his brain, and caused him a rather considerable twinge of conscience. No doubt she was only a friend in the precise acceptation of the term: no words of love had ever entered into their many long conversations, neither had he employed towards her that indescribable but nevertheless very comprehensible language of the eyes, in which one look may be made to do service for a whole sentence. And yet, somehow or other, he felt decidedly uncomfortable as those reflections passed rapidly through his mind; and he seemed to see the glance of very peculiar import with which Miss Crewe would receive the tidings that he had plighted his faith to Miss de Burgh, more particularly as their mutual bearing quite recently was in no way calculated to prepare her for an announcement so very surprising.

All this, which has taken some time to write, occurred to him in an instant; but as he clasped the still shrinking Augusta in his arms, he resolutely dismissed the subject from his mind, and raising one white hand gently to his lips, he murmured in her not unwilling ear, "My dearest, it is you I love, and you only."

"Sir Charles, I cannot, I dare not believe you," said Augusta, faintly. "You are very kind, very good; but this must not be. Let this night be to us both as if it had never been; or, rather, let it be for us the commencement of a new and sincere friendship, that shall not be lightly shaken by trifles. We know each other better now; perhaps we did not do each other justice before; it will be different in the future: and now I must really go."

"Not till I have the pledge I want," replied Sir Charles, with gentle firmness. "Let us be friends if you will, I cordially agree to that part of the bargain; but there must be more than that, Augusta. You must promise to accept me and my love."

"No, no," murmured Augusta, "it cannot be, I cannot promise."

"Not if I beg you to grant me this great boon; if I tell you that your refusal will cause me deep and lasting sorrow?" urged Sir Charles; who, like many of his sex, began to desire the fulfilment of his petition all the more strongly that success appeared about to elude him. "You will not treat me so cruelly as this, Augusta—raising anticipations only to doom them to disappointment?"

"I cannot, cannot tell what to do!" said Augusta, wildly, as she put her hair back from her forehead, and tried to steady the beating of her pulses. "It is you who are cruel, Sir Charles, in speaking to me as you are doing now. You know the weakness of my heart, and through it you are seeking to lead me into a course that I feel to be wrong. Let me go while I have some strength, some self-respect left!"

"Not until you have promised," was his

reply, as he again wound his arm around her. "Is it so hard a thing, Augusta? You say you love me; will you not then promise to be my own dear wife? Say that you will, my dearest one—whisper it in my ear—one little word—yes!"

"Oh! Sir Charles! Sir Charles!" exclaimed the poor girl, yielding almost in spite of herself; "are you not deceiving me—do you really, truly wish it?"

"I do indeed, my darling," said Sir Charles, holding her closely to his heart; "really and truly; believe me when I say so."

"Then I will be your wife," she murmured, in a low tone; and she drooped forward as she said it, and hid her burning blushes on his breast.

It was over—they had pledged their faith to one another; and some moments of rapturous silence followed, unbroken by word from either. Augusta had reached the pinnacle of every earthly happiness; the only heart she cared to win had just bound itself to her for ever, was even now throbbing against her own; no more delicious moment had she ever known in all her bright and unclouded life; never again did she experience the same sensation of intoxicating joy, as in those first precious minutes of crowning and bewildering ecstasy.   For with time came reaction and reflection, and also the remembrance that this lover had not sought her of his own free will, but had in a manner been compelled by honourable motives and feelings to speak to her as he had done.

But he had told her he loved her—told her that he would have sought her long since but for her coldness and apparent indifference to him. Well, it might be so, it might: and Augusta hugged the consoling suggestion to her bosom, and resolved to stifle every doubt and misgiving in the bud, and accept now and for ever her strange and new-found happiness, prized all the more dearly that it had seemed to be on the point of eluding her grasp for ever.

They remained together but a short time

longer. More than an hour had elapsed since Miss de Burgh quitted the ball-room; and she felt that to prolong her absence would only give rise to unpleasant comments.

"Let us go," said Augusta. "I must return home," she added, faintly, for the excitement she had undergone had completely exhausted her.

Sir Charles led her towards the terrace; she leaning on his arm, and her trembling fingers locked in his firm grasp.

As they reached the steps he paused, and addressed her in lover-like tones:—"Now, dearest! I am going to scold you, though it may seem very early days for me to assume that privilege. Can you guess the cause?"

"No, I cannot," replied Augusta, timidly.

"You call me *Sir* Charles; and that is a thing that I cannot permit any longer. Promise me, my darling, that you will not repeat the offence."

"I will try not to do so," said Augusta, with a smile: "but I am scarcely accustomed to our 'relative positions' yet. Oh! Sir Charles, is it all true—shall you never regret what you have done? There is still time to retract all if you have any doubt."

"As you are not able to keep your own promise for half a minute, I must not feel too much hurt that you should doubt my power of keeping mine," replied Sir Charles, in a jesting tone. "What a little infidel it is!" and he raised the soft hand he held to his lips and kissed it with much fervour, saying as he did so—"Have no fear, my darling; I love you very dearly: and I trust neither of us shall ever have cause to repent this night's work."

Augusta felt that her inmost heart thrilled at his words and his touch: a soft and delicious languor stole over her, she could not even utter one syllable of response, but a faint pressure of the hand told Sir Charles that she understood and believed him, and they ascended the steps in silence.

A few paces further, and they came to an open window. It was the window through which Augusta had gazed on Sir Charles Bellingham and Miss Crewe as they sat there all unconscious of observation; and she glanced at her lover as they approached it to see if he remembered it too.

He did not, she saw that plainly enough: indeed, the room had nothing very particular to distinguish it from many similar ones in the palace; handsomely furnished, the walls covered with paintings, blazing with chandeliers, chairs and settees scattered here and there; that was all.

It was empty; and Sir Charles led Augusta into it, and by chance placed her in the very seat formerly occupied by Miss Crewe; without one thought of the chaos of emotions agitating the mind of his companion, causing her to feel as if all around her, herself included, were but the images and phantasmagoria of a dream.

"Will you remain here while I go and find my mother?" inquired Sir Charles, tenderly, as he saw the deathly paleness of her countenance revealed by the brilliant lamp-light. " You are not fit to encounter those hot crowded rooms, I can see that. Do you feel ill, my darling? You are very white." And he bent over her with real interest and affection.

Augusta, trembling and overcome by the variety of emotions she had undergone, had barely strength to reply, " Yes, I will remain here: I feel tired and faint, but I shall be better presently, when I get home."

" I hardly like to leave you," said Sir Charles, arranging a cushion behind her; " but I shall be back directly, and we shall lose no time in conveying you home."

He left her alone for a few minutes, and departed on his mission of looking for Lady Agnes. He had not the slightest difficulty in doing this: for the good lady occupied the same position in which he had seen her in the earlier part of the evening.

" Where have you been, Charles?" she exclaimed, as he rejoined her. " I am sure the carriage must have come, and I am quite ready to go."

" I am just going to inquire for it," replied
her son. "Miss de Burgh is not very well,
and wishes to return home. Their carriage
is not ordered till much later in the evening; so will you take her with you when
you go?"

" I shall be very glad to do so," said
Lady Agnes; " but I am sorry to hear she
is indisposed. She looked particularly well
when she arrived."

"I don't think it is anything very serious,"
replied Sir Charles, carelessly; " over-
fatigue, or something of that kind. She
will be all right when she is quietly at
home again. Now, I shall see about the
carriage, mother; and if it is there I shall
come and fetch you."

Presently he reappeared, and announced
that the carriage was in readiness. " I will
take you to the room where I left Miss de
Burgh," he continued, as he offered Lady
Agnes his arm. " She will not require to
come in here at all : we can go straight
out through the vestibule, and so into the
hall."

On their way, however, they encountered Sir John de Burgh.

"Have you seen my daughter?" he inquired. "I cannot find her: she has been absent from the ball-room for a considerable time."

"Miss de Burgh is resting in one of the side rooms," replied Sir Charles, trying hard to look unconcerned. "She feels fatigued, and my mother is on her way to offer to take her home, as our carriage is now ready."

"I am very much indebted to Lady Agnes," said Sir John, with his accustomed air of stately courtesy; "but I am sorry she should require to go out of her way. Had I been aware that Augusta wished to return home, I should have sent for the carriage directly."

"Ours was at the door, Sir John; and the little *détour* is not of the slightest importance," said Lady Agnes. "I shall see her safely home, and a night's rest will make all right."

But the kind old lady was greatly

shocked when she saw the excessive pallor and evident suffering of the poor girl who sat awaiting her. A heavy reaction had now set in for Augusta; and the wild look of her eyes and rigid expression of her white lips told the experienced judgment of Lady Agnes that this was no mere case of trifling over-exertion or indisposition consequent on crowded and heated rooms.

She took Augusta's hand gently in hers, and told her how grieved she was to find her suffering. "But you will come with me now, my dear; the carriage is quite ready; and once at home, I trust you will very soon recover."

A flood of colour rushed into the pale face of Augusta as she replied, "Thank you, Lady Agnes; you are very kind."

At this moment Sir John de Burgh, who had been stopped by a friend, entered the room. "I am sorry to hear you are not feeling well, my dear," he remarked, kindly. "As Lady Agnes is good enough to offer to take you home, I think you are wise to go; but I hope it is nothing of any importance. I am glad to see you don't look very ill."

For Augusta was all flushed with agitation now; and her father was rather justified in his observation.

"May I take you to the carriage?" said Sir John, offering his arm to Lady Agnes. "Can we get out this way?" turning towards the vestibule as he spoke.

"Perfectly well," replied Sir Charles, who was now conducting his *fiancée*; "that passage leads right to the outer hall."

There Sir John assisted Lady Agnes to assume some comfortable elderly-lady wrappings, and then handed her into the carriage.

Augusta's bright crimson burnous was now turned on one side, then on the other, by the unpractised hands of the new-made lover, till she laughingly showed him how to attire her, and a lovely blush rose to her cheek as her fingers touched his in the hurried attempt at fastening it.

"What! are you coming too, Charles?" said Lady Agnes, with great surprise, as her son, after handing in the fair invalid, entered the carriage himself, and assumed a seat just opposite her. "I fancied you would stay very late to-night; one of the last balls you will have!"

"My dear mother, you speak as if I were as devoted to balls as a young girl in her first season! I am not such an ardent disciple of Terpsichore; and I am going home now if you will allow me."

Sir John de Burgh had informed them he should remain till his own carriage came to fetch him; and when they drove off he returned to the scene of festivity.

There was not much conversation between Lady Agnes and her two companions as they drove rapidly through the deserted and badly-lighted streets. She was immersed in reflections that filled her mind with painful anxiety: the others had thoughts of their own that also fully occupied them, and no one felt particularly disposed to talk on indifferent subjects.

"I hope you will be much better by to-morrow morning, my dear," said Lady Agnes, as the carriage stopped at Sir John de Burgh's gate. "I shall send over to inquire as soon as I think you are up."

"I am sure I shall be quite well," replied Augusta, as she bade the old lady good night, and prepared to quit the carriage. "Thank you very much for all your kindness, dear Lady Agnes."

She spoke with more warmth than Lady Agnes had ever known her exhibit before; and moved partly by sympathy with her tone of feeling, partly by pity for the suffering that she had so recently undergone, the old lady bent forward and kissed her affectionately, saying as she did so, "Good night, my dear. I am very glad to have been of any service to you. I shall always be glad to do anything I can for you."

There was no time for more; the servant stood at the open carriage door, Sir Charles had jumped out, and was waiting just beyond.

Augusta gave him her hand, and assisting her to alight, he led her inside the court gate, and after an absence of a few moments he returned and resumed his place beside his mother.

"What does all this mean, Charles?" said Lady Agnes, after a short pause. "What caused that sudden attack of Miss de Burgh's? Her illness was mental, not bodily, as you tried to make me believe. You know what caused her agitation—what is the meaning of it?"

"It means, mother," and the young man hesitated, and seemed to find some difficulty in expressing himself; "well, it means, that in Miss de Burgh you see your future daughter-in-law, and my future wife."

Lady Agnes sat as one stunned, and uttered no word or sound. Often as this conclusion had presented itself to her mind as a thing not impossible, nor even very improbable; still, now that it had come upon her as a reality, a fact, she felt how little she had really been prepared for it—how utterly it was opposed to all the wishes and aspirations she had formed regarding her son.

"Is this true?" she said, in a low tone,

rousing herself from a lengthened reverie; "is it quite true, Charles?"

"It is quite true, mother," replied Sir Charles gently; "Augusta de Burgh is my promised wife."

The carriage stopped as he spoke, and no further remark was made on either side.

Sir Charles handed his mother into the house, and led her into the *salon.* "You can go, Carson," she said, addressing her maid, who waited to attend her mistress; "I will come presently." The woman retired and closed the door behind her.

With trembling fingers Lady Agnes put aside the cloak in which she had been wrapped; then turning to Sir Charles, who stood doubtful and irresolute, she laid her hands gently on his shoulders, and looked with earnest and tender scrutiny into his eyes.

"It is true, Charles; and you love her?"

"It is true, mother; and I love her," he replied, rather averting his glance from her steadfast gaze; "and, mother, you will love her, you will try to love her, too.   For my sake you will try to receive her as a daughter."

"I will do so, Charles. As she is a true and loving wife to you, so shall she be a cherished daughter to me. God bless you, my son, my only son!—and God bless her too, for your sake!"

Sir Charles drew his mother fondly towards him, and she hid her tearful face on his shoulder. Both were very deeply moved; Sir Charles not less so than Lady Agnes. For the moment had come to those two long and tenderly attached hearts, when a mother's love and a mother's sacred influence could no longer claim the first and highest place in the affections of her son. That position would belong of right to his wife now: God grant that she may hold it as purely and faithfully as the tried and noble parent, whose duty to her child has only yielded in sacredness to her duty to her Maker.

"You will tell me more to-morrow," said Lady Agnes at length, gently disengaging herself from her son's embrace.

"It is late now, and I must think over what I have heard. It has taken me by surprise I own; surely it is somewhat sudden, Charles; but I shall ask no questions to-night, I shall hear all in the morning. Good night, my own dear boy; God for ever bless and keep you!"

Once more she imprinted a tender kiss on his frank and open brow: and with a long lingering look of pride and affection at the son whom she had ever found so loving and dutiful, Lady Agnes quitted the apartment and left him to his reflections. Sir Charles paced up and down for some minutes, whistling a tune very softly to himself as he did so. Presently he stopped, and laughed a little laugh that had no particular merriment in it.

"'Love's Young Dream!'" he muttered to himself: "it is odd enough that of all songs in the world that especial one should have suggested itself at this precise moment. It was no thought of mine, I am sure: a curious coincidence I suppose. Well, well! the sooner I can bring myself to regard it as 'love's young dream' the better; for it is all the dream I am ever likely to have. I am fairly in for it now, not a doubt on that subject." He continued his quarter-deck promenade, and also resumed the Irish melody.

"How handsome she looked to-night! By far the handsomest woman I ever saw: there's something in that. One must feel proud of owning such a glorious creature: a beautiful wife is a very pleasant possession. And her unaffected distress, her tears; they gave me a sensation of tugging at my very heartstrings. I should have been a brute had I not acted as I did: it was a case of perfectly plain-sailing, the course marked out as distinctly as possible."

Another turn or two, the tune now being the "Bay of Biscay," probably suggested by the nautical tendency of the young baronet's final reflection.

"It was very noble of her too, wishing to let me off as she did; she has very high feelings, one can see that. How grand she looked when she declined to take advantage of my offer! I like a woman who shows a proper spirit. I believe I am more than half in love with her already—no saying but it may be a desperate attachment yet. Somebody says somewhere that in matrimony it is best to start with a little aversion. We may be a perfect case of Darby and Joan, who knows?" and the whistling of "Love's Young Dream" was recommenced with much vigour.

"Miss Crewe—ahem! I wonder how the fair Emily will take it ? Rather an unexpected termination to her little fairy tale;" and Sir Charles could not help laughing with tolerable heartiness as he recalled the legend of the fairy godmother. " The beautiful young lady retained the handkerchief after all," he exclaimed, suddenly. " Well, well! I suppose it was so fated." Having arrived at this conclusion, Sir Charles lit a candle and proceeded to a small den he had especially devoted to his own pursuits, and where he was wont to refresh himself occasionally with the soothing influence of a cigar.

CHAPTER V.

Much more than an hour had elapsed since
Augusta de Burgh dismissed her maid;
and she still lingered by the fire in her
dressing-room, gazing with a mournful and
fixed intensity on the smouldering embers,
and seeing strange forms and faces in their
glowing depths.

A loose wrapper of lustrous crimson silk
contrasted well with the transparent purity
of her skin, and with the waving masses of
her dark glossy hair, which in all its rich
profusion streamed down over neck and
shoulders, and half-hid face and figure in a
dusky veil.

Rich attire, jewels, all were laid aside;
and yet she looked far more beautiful and
winning than when robed in her costliest

array, and shining with gems that might have graced the coronet of a queen. As she sat there in her low chair by the side of the fire, her thoughts travelled back over every hour and moment of that eventful evening, and then wandered forward to the future, that unknown, untried future, that was now for her filled with visions of too great, too transcendent felicity. Quarter after quarter rung on the chimes of the little French time-piece above her head; and yet Augusta reclined listlessly against the silken cushions, and let her thoughts linger at their own free will on each brilliant image that presented itself to her imagination.

Doubts and misgivings she felt, too, at times; and then her face would cloud over, and the light would fade out of her dark dreamy eyes; but she put those resolutely aside, and resolved to believe in the reality of the happiness now apparently so firmly within her grasp.

"For he *shall* love me!" she whispered to herself; and all alone as she was, the rich colour mantled over cheek and brow. "I will love him so that every fibre of his being shall respond to it. People call me cold!" and a faintly sarcastic smile hovered on her lip for a moment; "they little know me! they little dream what is here!" clasping her hands tightly on her bosom as she spoke. "But he shall know; and if he loves me now, as he tells me he does, he shall ere long know what is the true meaning of the word. No one yet has ever dreamt of how Augusta de Burgh can love —ay, and can *hate*, too, if need be. I fancy I should make rather a dangerous enemy, if my indignation were once thoroughly roused. Those who love strongly generally hate pretty strongly too." Her thoughts just glanced at the smiling countenance and sunny tresses of Miss Crewe; and we feel bound to confess that her reflections at the moment were not precisely of the nature of that charity that "thinketh no evil."

Next morning arose bright and beaming on all the various personages of our tale.

Miss de Burgh was late, but no traces of the agitation of the preceding night were visible in her appearance as she entered the breakfast-room.

"I need not ask how you are, my dear," said her father, as he rose to receive her; " your look is sufficient to relieve my mind of all uneasiness. There are some letters for you," he added, pushing several in the direction of his daughter. "I have one from England, from Mr. Talbot: but it seems lengthy, so I have postponed its perusal."

They continued their meal in silence: Sir John had unfolded the *Times*, and was absorbed in its ample sheet; while Augusta read her letters, and once or twice wondered what Sir Charles Bellingham was about, and when he would arrive, as he said he should, to lay his proposal before the father of his *fiancée*.

Presently, the *Times* having been thoroughly scanned, Sir John laid it aside, and took up his letters.

"Ah! by the way, Mr. Talbot's. I may as well read it now."

Scarcely had he read the first few sentences when his brow darkened into an angry frown, an exclamation of surprised displeasure escaped him, and he brought his hand down heavily on the table.

"What is it, papa?" inquired Augusta, much astonished.

"Some absurd notion this old fool has got into his head! Wanting to bring her here, indeed! I must write instantly and forbid it."

"Bring whom, papa? What has annoyed you in Mr. Talbot's letter?"

"He wishes to bring that girl here—your sister Marian," replied Sir John, rather wincing at the latter part of his sentence.

"Why should he bring her here?" asked Augusta; "what is his reason for proposing such a thing?"

"There is his letter, you can read it for yourself," said her father, handing her the closely-written sheet which he had just glanced through. "Some nonsensical love affair seems to be at the bottom of it: they should have taken better care whom they put in her way, and must take the consequences now.   All I know is that she shall not come here.   Bring me the letter when you have finished it, as I must answer it by to-day's post."   So saying he rose from table, and with a very gloomy expression took his departure to his own particular sanctum. Augusta read Mr. Talbot's letter calmly through, and then she re-perused it even more carefully.   In conclusion she folded it up slowly and meditatively, and she too rose and quitted the room; but she did not at once proceed in search of her father. For, at the moment when she had read the last line, there came a resonant peal at the hall bell: and the tell-tale colour in Miss de Burgh's cheek told that she had a pretty shrewd guess as to who the early visitor might be.   Therefore she sought the seclusion of her own boudoir, and there awaited the result of the all-important interview.

She had not long to linger in suspense; for, in a shorter time than she could have imagined possible, she heard voices on the staircase; and directly afterwards a servant knocked at her door, and informed her that her presence was desired by Sir John de Burgh in his study.

With a beating heart Augusta obeyed the summons; and as she entered her father's apartment she glanced anxiously at his impassive countenance, in which no token of approval or disapproval was to be discovered.

"Take a chair, Augusta," he said, rather gravely, "I have something to say to you."

She seated herself in the place to which he directed her: and as she did so Sir John assumed the Englishman's position in front of the fire-place, though the morning was bright and sunny, and the logs remained unlighted in the grate.

"You probably guess why I have sent for you," he began, after a short pause to arrange his ideas. "I have had a visitor just now," he continued, "whose errand I believe is not unknown to you—Sir Charles Bellingham. You were aware that he was coming, Augusta?"

"Yes, papa," she replied, in a low tone, blushing painfully at the same time.

"I was not at all prepared for his communication," observed Sir John, calmly. "When last we spoke on this subject, Augusta, you led me to form a very different conclusion. This was, if I am not mistaken, barely two days ago; so the change in your sentiments has certainly been tolerably rapid. May I ask if you seriously desire to become the wife of Sir Charles Bellingham?"

"If you have no objection, papa," said Augusta, with a hurried glance at his grave countenance.

"I can have no tangible grounds for objecting," replied her father, "if you have really made up your mind on the subject. Sir Charles Bellingham is in no way ineligible: his family is very good, his fortune a very handsome one: so far as those points are concerned there is not a word to be said."

He paused, as if expecting a reply; but Augusta said nothing.

Sir John cleared his throat once or twice, and yet when he spoke again his voice was thick and husky.

"We have not had occasion to speak much on this subject before, Augusta: you have had suitors, I know; their acceptance or rejection I left entirely to yourself, feeling that in such a matter you had every right to full confidence at my hands. But there are particular circumstances in this case that induce me to act differently. I am ignorant of what has passed between Sir Charles and yourself: perhaps I have been less watchful in such a matter than the father of a motherless girl was called upon to be." As he said this he turned towards the empty fire-place, and remained silent for two or three minutes : and Augusta knew that he was thinking of his dead wife, and mourning the absence of the fond mother who would have known so well how to shield and protect her daughter. Presently he resumed his remarks.

"Augusta," he said, gently, "you know how early I lost your mother, you know how I have mourned her: but neither you nor any one else can ever know what her loss was to me, what a life of perfect love and happiness was for ever quenched by that blow; even now it pains me, pains me deeply to recall those happy days: but it is the recollection of them and of my dear dead wife that urges me to speak to you as I am now doing. Why are you marrying this man, Augusta? But a few short hours since you told me you were nothing to each other, that it was mere idle tattle that connected your name with his; then what is the meaning of this change? · If you do not love him—if you do not feel for him as a woman should feel towards her husband, then do not seek to become his wife. Let no consideration induce you to enter on a course that can only entail on you lasting disappointment and misery."

"I—I love him, papa," replied Augusta, in so low a voice as to be scarcely audible; and she hid her burning cheeks in her hands.

There was perfect silence for some minutes between the father and daughter. Augusta's whole frame quivered with agitation; and Sir John stood observing her narrowly, till by degrees all the hardness had gone out of his countenance, and a look of pitying tenderness alone remained; a look that for many a long year had not rested on those grave impassive features.

"You say you love Sir Charles Bellingham, Augusta," he continued very gently. "Such a declaration ought certainly to quiet all my doubts and scruples; but I am not yet entirely satisfied. Your happiness is at stake, and that is no light matter in my eyes. Does he also love you? This may appear an unnecessary question, when scarcely an hour ago he asked my consent to his marriage with you; but those reports and rumours which reached my ears may also have reached his, and may have impelled him to a course he had not otherwise contemplated. I fear I may give you pain by such remarks, my dear Augusta," and Sir John made a step or two forward, and laid his hand very softly on the drooping young head still buried in the trembling hands. He could not see how pallid and contracted her features became as she listened to him, nor yet could he know the keen pang of agony that like a strong grasp seemed to clutch convulsively at her heart; so he continued in a kind and earnest voice, " This subject shall never again be named between us; I would not willingly speak as I am doing now, but that your future happiness is more to me than mere feelings of ceremony or false delicacy. Does this young man love you as I would have my daughter loved by the man she chooses for her husband, as you would wish to be loved yourself, Augusta? Or has a generous principle of honour induced him to solicit the hand of a woman whose name has been so far compromised by his thoughtless and meaningless attentions that it has been unjustifiably linked with his, and has for a time formed the subject of idle gossip and slander? If it be so, if he has not chosen you frankly and freely, of his own will and unbiassed by any ulterior motive—do not accept him, Augusta, not even if you love him yourself. It will bring you no happiness; believe me, my dear girl, when I tell you so."

"He loves me, papa—he has told me that he does," replied Augusta, in a faltering tone, as she writhed beneath the cruel anguish his observations caused her. "He had never heard the reports to which you allude; or if he had, they have nothing to do with his proposal."

"Then I have nothing further to say, my dear," said Sir John, in a voice of satisfaction; "and you have my willing consent to your marriage. May all happiness attend you, my child;" and he embraced her affectionately as he said so. "Be such a wife as was your angel mother, and Sir Charles will have good cause to bless me for the gift I am bestowing on him. Before very long, I doubt not, he will be here to receive his answer; though I fancy, so far as regards yourself, he knows it pretty well already. And now to reply to this letter of Mr. Talbot's. Have you finished reading it?"

"Yes, papa," said Augusta, with a slight hesitation in her manner. Sir John looked at her inquiringly; timidity and uncertainty of speech were new phases in the demeanour of his stately elder daughter.

"I have been thinking, papa——" and Augusta paused and gazed at him anxiously; "I think, perhaps, if you did not object very much, that it might be better to let my sister come here."

"Why on earth should she come here?" replied Sir John, his brow darkening as he spoke.

Augusta still hesitated.

"Some day, papa, you surely mean to see her and receive her home; if Mr. and Mrs. Talbot were dead she has no home but yours; you would not reject her in such a case?"

"Time enough when that happens," said Sir John, gloomily.

"They clearly wish you to take her now," replied Augusta; "and is not this a good opportunity to do so, papa? When I leave you she might supply my place. Parting from you is a very bitter thought to me; but if I left you quite alone the trial would be much harder. Were Marian with you I should feel happier; I should indeed, papa."

As she named her sister Sir John winced keenly for a moment, and words seemed starting to his lips, but he refrained from uttering them.

"She is your daughter, papa, as well as myself," urged Augusta, who saw that her remonstrances were producing an effect; "and she is my only sister. I should like to have her with me for a little while before I leave home; I should like her to be here when I am married; it is only right that she should be with us then."

"Her presence will be very painful to me, Augusta; you do not know how painful."

"Just at first you may feel it so, papa; but some day or other it must come to you, for you cannot desert her altogether. It will soon wear off, and you will become accustomed to her."

Sir John paced the apartment in silence for a few minutes.

"I will think over what you have said, Augusta," he remarked after an interval. "I certainly never contemplated this, and your suggestion has taken me by surprise."

"I do not wish to pain or annoy you, papa," said Augusta; "but people have commented on my sister's continued absence, and this will put an end to unpleasant remarks. Mr. and Mrs. Talbot would perhaps accompany her here, and remain till—till I am married." She blushed slightly at the latter part of her sentence.

"I do not in the least mind what people say or think of me," replied Sir John, haughtily; "I am the best judge of my own actions. If I consent to have your sister here it will be because it is your wish, Augusta: but I must have time for reflection. I shall not answer Mr. Talbot's letter until to-morrow, when I shall inform you of my decision. As to Sir Charles, I promised to let him know the result of my interview with you," he added. "I conclude I may invite him to make his appearance here whenever he pleases?"

"You will know what to say, papa," replied Miss de Burgh, with a slight increase of colour; "I shall leave you now, and not disturb you any longer."

"Very well, my dear," said her father, beginning to write; and Augusta swept gracefully across the apartment, and once more sought the solitude of her boudoir, there to await the arrival of her now affianced lover.

Before much time had elapsed he was by her side. He had already had a long interview with Lady Agnes, who had spent the greater portion of the night in anxious meditation respecting the future of her beloved son.

Rendered more than usually acute by her devoted solicitude for her only child, the fond mother could not avoid perceiving that something of mystery hung round his engagement to Miss de Burgh. What it might be she could not guess, and it was evident that Sir Charles had no intention of enlightening her. But the fact was there; he had avowed it with his own lips: Augusta was his promised wife, and the future mistress of Bellingham Park; all that now remained for Lady Agnes was to recognise that such was the case, and to receive the young lady with as much cordiality as was possible under the circumstances.

So, when Sir Charles for the second time took his way to the house of his lady-love, Lady Agnes accompanied him; remaining in the carriage for a few minutes, that her son might apprise the young lady of her visit, and prepare her for a meeting naturally so important to them both. It passed off well. Augusta, under the influence of conflicting emotions of love and a timid consciousness, was softer and more subdued than she had ever appeared before : she looked radiantly lovely; and as Lady Agnes noticed the graceful pose of her magnificent figure, and her eyes dwelt eagerly on her faultless features and glowing complexion, she ceased to wonder that her son should, as she imagined, have become enslaved by a beauty so bewitching, and blamed herself for her reluctance to be pleased with a marriage in which the bride seemed almost too richly endowed with the most lavish gifts of earthly fortune. The old lady embraced the fair *fiancée* with warm affection; saying, as she did so, many words of kind and tender interest. Augusta felt touched by her evident sincerity, and responded with a cordiality very unusual in one generally so reserved in her expression of feeling. Both ladies were agreeably disappointed in the result of their interview; and when Sir John de Burgh joined them, as he did shortly afterwards, he found an air of perfect harmony pervading their manner and conversation that surprised as much as it gratified him; for he had been rather doubtful of the reception Lady Agnes might accord to her future daughter-in-law. His invitation to the mother and son to dine with him that day was willingly acceded to; and they parted, to meet again at dinner-time, with a warmth and cordiality none of them had thought it possible they should experience only a few hours previously.

CHAPTER VI.

LATER in the afternoon of the same day Miss Crewe was seated in the pretty *salon* of the apartments occupied by her sister and herself in the Piazza di Spagna. Mrs. Greville had been out for some time, and had not yet returned from her walk; but Emily felt lazy, and made a trifling cold serve as an excuse for remaining at home; perhaps a particularly exciting novel which had just arrived from the library may have had some slight share in increasing the young lady's indisposition.

The wind was rather sharp, moreover; and Emily's was a disposition that eschewed cold, and loved warmth and sunshine. She had drawn a low chair in front of the sparkling wood fire, and had wrapped one of those brilliant Roman scarves comfortably round her shoulders; and she looked most thoroughly and enjoyably at her ease, and as if she would not have been at all obliged to any one who should disturb her in her pleasant and engrossing occupation.

Nevertheless, when the door was rather hastily thrown open, and her sister Norah entered the room with glowing cheeks, and eyes sparkling with evident excitement, Emily roused herself from the perusal of the novel; and laying the open page on her lap, she looked up half smiling at Mrs. Greville, who was just untying her bonnet-strings preparatory to discharging herself of her news.

"Well, Norah, what is it? You are clearly on the point of exploding with something or other. What great event is going to happen?"

"Oh! Emily, you'll be so surprised!"

"Shall I, dear? What can it be? It takes a good deal to surprise me now-a-days."

"But you will be surprised at this; at least I think so; I know I was. Not but what I once thought it a likely enough thing to happen, but not lately. And it is quite true."

"Well, let me hear what it is, dear; and then I will tell you if I think it so amazing."

"It is a marriage, Emily; can't you guess whose?" and Mrs. Greville glanced rather keenly at her sister.

"A marriage, Norah; let me think who it can be;" and she folded her hands together and gazed reflectively into the blazing embers. "I can't in the least guess," she remarked, after a short pause; "it doesn't seem to me that any particularly suspicious-looking flirtation has been going on of late."

"Perhaps not a flirtation, Emily; but can't you remember any two people who were certainly at one time a good deal taken up with each other?"

"I really can't, dear," replied Miss Crewe, after an instant of meditation; "everybody has been as good as gold this season; I can't imagine how a real live marriage can have been evolved from such very unpromising materials. So now solve the riddle, and name the victims."

Something seemed to have become en-
tangled among Mrs. Greville's many bracelets, for she twisted them round and round
for a minute without speaking.

"Friends of our own, Emily," she observed, with some hesitation, still keeping
her eyes fixed on her bracelets; "intimate
friends. Surely you can guess now."

"Why all this circumlocution, Norah?"
said Emily, now fairly sitting up and looking steadily at her sister: "why don't you
tell me at once who it is? I have not the
least idea who it can be."

"Miss de Burgh and Sir Charles Bellingham," replied Mrs. Greville, summoning
up all her courage for the decisive stroke.

"Nonsense!" said Miss Crewe, with resolution and some little scorn: "how can
you believe anything half so absurd, Norah?"
She threw herself back in her chair as she
uttered the words; and her ruby lip curled
with amused derision.

"It is not nonsense, Emily," continued
Mrs. Greville, with steady firmness; "it is
quite true."

"I know it is not, my dear," persisted Emily, still smiling in her fancied superior knowledge.

"But it is," repeated her sister, "quite, quite true; I have it from the best authority."

"Whose authority, Norah?" and there was a faint sneer in the tone of Miss Crewe's voice.

"I do not usually spread unfounded reports, Emily," replied Mrs. Greville, at last slightly nettled by her sister's manner. "The person who told me was Sir John de Burgh."

"Norah!" and Emily again sat up and faced her sister, with a strange light in her eye, and a deepening colour in her cheek; "is this a fact that you are telling me; for I can scarcely credit it even yet?"

"I thought it would surprise you," replied Mrs. Greville, in a tone of satisfaction; "it is quite a fact; for I met Sir John in Monaldini's just before I came home, and he told me all about it directly. He said he was sure we should feel interested in hearing of it, as we knew his daughter and her future husband so well. Those were his very words."

"Her future husband!" muttered Emily, between her closed lips; "am I awake or dreaming? the thing is an utter mystery to me!"

Mrs. Greville did not catch what she said, but she saw that her sister was much excited by the intelligence she had just received, and a new feeling of uneasiness took possession of her warm Irish heart.

"Surely she did not love him herself!" was her hasty mental reflection; "I am sure I warned her over and over again that she was foolish in talking and sitting with Sir Charles as she did, and he but amusing himself with her after all."

"Well, Norah!" said Emily, at length, speaking as if it were rather an effort to do so; "I must allow that your news has fairly taken me by surprise. I should not have guessed it in a twelvemonth."

"It hasn't vexed you, dear, has it?" replied her sister, kindly; coming at the same time to the back of Emily's chair, and fondly stroking the rich glossy braids of her hair. "You are not disappointed that he is going to marry Miss de Burgh?"

"It is no disappointment to me, so far as regards myself, Norah; don't let any idea of that kind take possession of your dear old head:" and Miss Crewe drew down the sweet womanly face that gazed on her so anxiously, and imprinted a very affectionate kiss on the full bright lips. "But in some sense it is a disappointment, dear; I don't intend to deny that. You know what I think of Sir Charles Bellingham, and what I think of Miss de Burgh; she is not good enough for him, Norah, and they are not at all suited to each other. I know that; and I know they wont be happy together."

"How can you tell that, Emily? If they love each other, they must be happy."

"Very true, if they love each other; but there's just the difficulty. I don't imagine that Sir Charles Bellingham has any very desperate attachment to Miss de Burgh. I may be wrong, Norah, but I don't think it."

"Oh! Emily, when he has asked her to marry him!"

"When can he possibly have done it?" said Miss Crewe, musingly. "Last night they were barely civil to each other; he almost entirely neglected her, forgot his engagement to dance with her—I cannot make it out! They were not engaged then: of that I am certain."

All farther comments were cut short by the opening of the door, and by the unexpected announcement of no less a visitor than Sir Charles Bellingham himself.

Considerable embarrassment was clearly visible in the manner of every member of the trio. Sir Charles did not enter with his ordinary air of familiar " at-home-ish-ness," but in a much quieter and more ceremonious way than was at all usual with him: and he rather avoided meeting the eyes of both ladies as he shook hands with them. Mrs. Greville looked as if she felt that if running out of the room had been at all practicable in the circumstances, it would have been the course most consonant with her inclinations. Miss Crewe was decidedly the least disturbed of the group; but even she could not restrain a warmer tint than common from mounting into her fair cheek, while at the same time she was conscious that her greeting betrayed a slight amount of stiffness, which she would have carefully subdued had but a few moments of preparation been afforded her.

Some trifling comments on the weather formed the first rather constrained subject of conversation : and Mrs. Greville, who had been twirling her bonnet-strings round her fingers in an agony of indecision, took instant advantage of the opening to remark that she had just returned from her walk, and must go and take off her things.

Scarcely had the door closed behind her than Sir Charles, who had previously been leaning against the mantel-piece, took a chair nearer Miss Crewe, and began at once without the slightest circumlocution, "I see by your manner, Miss Crewe, that you have already heard what I have come to tell you."

"Norah was just telling me some gossip about you when you came in," replied the young lady, carelessly; "but I don't generally put much faith in the reports one constantly hears, and this one seemed to me rather more absurd than usual."

"I know you must have felt much surprised, Miss Crewe," said Sir Charles, looking down for a moment: "but had it been a mere idle report you should not have seen me here now, at least not on my present errand. I am come to announce to you my engagement to Miss de Burgh; and I much wish that I had been the first to tell you of it. I thought I should have been so."

"I can't echo your wish, Sir Charles," replied Emily, smiling, "because it would have deprived Norah of the enjoyment of my look of unqualified amazement at her news. So it is really true!" and she looked him full in the face for a moment, with a bright smile, in which might be read

also the least little touch of scorn: "well,
I conclude, I must offer you my best congratulations, and wish you joy on your
approaching marriage. That is the proper
thing to do, I think."

"Thanks for your good wishes, Miss
Crewe," said the young baronet, quietly;
and for a few moments there was rather an
awkward pause.

"You have not been riding to-day, I
suppose?" observed Emily, at length; "it
was so very cold."

"No, I did not ride," said Sir Charles,
in an absent manner; "I had not much
time to do so;" and rather an amused smile
flitted across his handsome features.

"What is to be said or done now?" was
Miss Crewe's mental reflection; but she
only leant back in her chair, and held her
embroidered handkerchief up by two
corners, while she carefully studied its
flowery pattern; rather a favourite occupation with ladies when resolutely determined
that an unfortunate man shall struggle out
of an embarrassing predicament as best he

may, perfectly unaided by any help that they can afford him."

Therefore, Sir Charles, seeing pretty clearly the position of affairs, made up his mind to lose no more time in beating about the bush; but boldly, and without further hesitation, to plunge into the middle of the subject.   The extended handkerchief gave him a valuable opportunity, of which he forthwith availed himself.

"That pretty fairy tale which you told me the other evening, Miss Crewe; you will now be able to supply the missing pages."

"Shall I, Sir Charles?   Oh! of course. The beautiful young lady retained possession of the magic handkerchief; and she and the prince were soon afterwards married, and lived happily all the rest of their days."

"I hope they did," said Sir Charles, and he glanced at his fair companion with an expression half appealing, half comic; "I hope they did, Miss Crewe."

"No doubt of it," replied Emily, returning his glance; "fairy tales always end happily."

"Ah! Miss Crewe, say that you hope this of mine will! Wish me joy more sincerely than you did a minute ago."

Voice, look, manner, all were changed: eagerness and sincerity were written on every feature of Sir Charles's countenance, as he now cast away all affectation and reserve, and gazed anxiously on the still impassive face of Emily Crewe.

"Did you not consider my congratulations sincere, Sir Charles? How do you know they were not?" and Emily suspended her examination of the handkerchief, and looked at him with great composure.

"One generally has an instinct as regards these matters, Miss Crewe; and I don't think you were quite sincere in your congratulations just now."

"We will waive the discussion of that question for the present, Sir Charles; and I, for my part, will ask you if you can expect me to give you a first-class certificate for honesty and straightforwardness of conduct?"

"You may think you cannot, Miss Crewe; but if all were known, you might fairly do so. We must not always judge from appearances in this world; and the present case is one in which you may safely reserve your opinion."

Emily remained silent; but her look invited a further confidence, if Sir Charles were disposed to afford it.

"We have been very good friends, Miss Crewe," continued Sir Charles, after a moment's pause for her reply; "do not let a light cause disturb that friendship now. I am aware that the announcement of my engagement to Miss de Burgh must naturally have taken you considerably by surprise, especially when taken in conjunction with various circumstances much opposed to such a conclusion. I came here to-day to inform you of this engagement myself: for I felt that after our recent conversation at Lord A——'s, you could scarcely avoid the conviction that I had been intentionally misleading you. That I have not done so, Miss Crewe, you may believe. When I spoke to you that evening at Lord A——'s, and also at the ball last night, Miss de Burgh and I were nothing to each other, in so far, at least, as regards any suspicion of the tie that unites us now. We are now solemnly bound to each other; she is my promised wife; and her interests and mine from henceforward are one. I am aware that she has not been a favourite of yours, Miss Crewe; but I hope, for my sake, that you will try to like her for the future. She has a noble and generous heart, believe me; her coldness is merely on the surface, there are very warm feelings beneath."

"Love, if this be love, must be a trifle blinder than usual in his case," mused Miss Emily to herself. "Augusta de Burgh generous, noble, warm-hearted! The man must be dreaming! A sad awakening it will be when he finds what she really is."

But Emily was frank and generous to a fault; and recognising as she did that she had allowed herself to be betrayed into an unwarrantable display of annoyance, she now hastened to repair her error and atone for the hasty ebullition into which she had been led by her warm Irish nature and genuine openness of disposition.

"Not another word, Sir Charles!" she frankly exclaimed; "I cry 'peccavi' on my bended knees, if you will have it so. We shall be the firm friends we have ever been, and Miss de Burgh shall be included in our bond of union. I wont deny that hitherto I have not specially affected her; but that may be, as you say, because I don't know her as she really is. As your future wife I shall view her very differently: and now, Sir Charles, from the very bottom of my heart I sincerely wish you every happiness this world can bestow. You will accept my congratulations now, wont you?"

She held out both her hands towards him as she finished speaking, while her lovely features shone with an expression of deep interest and regard; nay, something very like a tear glistened in her bright eyes as she raised them to the face of the young man for whom she felt so true a friendship

—a feeling such as she might have experienced towards a brother. had she ever
possessed one.

Sir Charles, on his part, was not slow to
respond to her change of mood. He clasped
the soft white hands in his, and raising one
of them to his lips, he imprinted on it a
kiss rather more tender in its character
than his beautiful betrothed would have
been at all likely to approve of had she
witnessed the performance.

"Come, come, Sir Charles! I must call
you to order," said Emily, in a gay voice,
while a faint blush stole over cheek and
brow. "I suppose you think that because
you are in Italy you may follow the Italian
customs; but you must remember you are
no longer a free agent now, but have devoted yourself, heart and soul, to the
service of one liege lady. And now tell
me when this mighty event is to come off;
though it is perhaps rather early days to
be discussing time and place."

"Well, neither has yet been alluded
to," replied Sir Charles, rather sheepishly;

"but I believe all matters of this nature are in the province of the lady."

"Sir John de Burgh has a beautiful property in England," observed Emily; "that would be the most natural place for the marriage to be celebrated. Don't you think so?"

"I am not sure," replied Sir Charles, reflectively. "You see they have been so long absent from their English home that the people thereabouts are all almost strangers to them. That would not be so pleasant."

"But they must have relations in England," urged Miss Crewe: "the youngest Miss de Burgh is there, and the grandfather and grandmother who have brought her up."

"I know Augusta wishes her sister to come out here," said Sir Charles; "she told me so this afternoon. Her father dreads the meeting, because the mother, whom he idolized, died at Marian's birth; and he has heard that this daughter strongly resembles her."

" It seems rather a strange way of showing affection for a dead wife, entirely to neglect her poor motherless child," observed Emily, rather indignantly. " Poor little thing! hers has been a sad fate ; if she does come here we must all be very good to her. It will be rather a trying ordeal for her under all the circumstances."

At this juncture Mrs. Greville entered the room rather nervously, for she had a strong dread that she might be interrupting some discussion in which her absence would be more desirable than her presence.

Had such appeared the case she had prepared a skilfully strategic retreat; but far from finding such a plan of operations at all necessary, her sister and her visitor seemed to. be on the best and easiest of terms; the conversation was not even interrupted on her entrance, though Sir Charles hastened to place a seat for her near the fire, and then proceeded to resume his own in its immediate vicinity.

Norah joined with much interest in the comments on the arrival of the younger Miss de Burgh: and then, finding further reticence unnecessary, she very heartily congratulated Sir Charles on his approaching marriage, and added her best wishes to those he had already received from her sister. We shall now leave them for the present, and return to some other personages of our tale, whose history has for a considerable time been neglected.

CHAPTER VII.

DEPARTURE FROM SUMMERTON.

It has been wet weather, and the roads around Summerton are muddy and heavy for walking; this I conclude is the postman's excuse for being so unusually late as he is this morning. Mr. Talbot has missed his daily paper; and more on his account than on her own, Marian de Burgh is straining her bright eyes through the misty pane, and tapping impatiently with her pretty white fingers on the old oak carving of its framework.

"There he is, grandpapa! I see him coming round the corner;" and heedless of the proprieties and the outraged feelings of the wheezy old butler, whose slow decorous progress could by no means keep pace with the nimble steps of his young mistress, Marian hastily quitted the room, and betook herself to the hall door, there to wait the all-important arrival of the postman and his bag of letters.

"Why, Jonas, how late you are! Grandpapa is quite wearying for his paper; but I suppose the roads are very heavy to-day."

"That they be, miss; and my legs are heavy enough too, carrying all the dirt that 'ud stick to them with no good will o' mine." And old Jonas glanced ruefully at his mud-bespattered leggings, which gave ample token of miry roads and hard trudging through them.

Voice or look must have conveyed some slight intimation to Mr. Talbot's pretty granddaughter; for she smiled kindly on the old postman, and as she took the Summerton bag from his hands, she bade him go round to the servants' entrance and thaw his frozen fingers at the hall fire; "and I shall tell them to give you a good glass of ale before you set out again," she added, with a little friendly nod as he retreated to obey her orders, and she closed the heavy oak door against the penetrating blast.

Mr. Talbot unlocked the bag, and handed forth its welcome contents. " A letter for me, actually!" exclaimed Marian, as she received one from her grandfather: "and from Augusta! Oh, grandpapa!" Her eager eyes were raised to his face, while her sweet countenance crimsoned over, and the hand that held the letter fell tremblingly by her side.

" Are you not going to open it?" said Mr. Talbot, encouragingly; "it is a long time since you have heard from your sister."

" Very long," replied Marian, in a sad tone, as she proceeded to fumble with the thin crackling paper.

" One from your papa, too," observed Mr. Talbot. " Come, Marian, this looks well, I think."

There was rather a long preamble in the commencement of Sir John de Burgh's somewhat lengthy effusion; and before Mr. Talbot had arrived at the gist of the

matter he was interrupted by an exclamation from Marian.

"Grandpapa, only think; Augusta is
going to be married!"

Still, with flushing cheeks and kindling
eyes, she hastily glanced over the closely-
written sheet; until, suddenly throwing herself into her grandfather's arms, she burst
into a choking fit of sobs, at the same time
murmuring in broken accents, " Oh, grandpapa! I am to go; I am to go!"

"Hush, my darling; don't cry so," said
Mr. Talbot, soothingly, as he clasped her
tenderly to his heart. "It is all right
now, and we shall take you to them ourselves. Don't cry any more; but dry your
eyes, and tell me what Augusta says. She
is going to be married, is she? Who is the
happy man?"

Diverted from her first keen emotions,
Marian raised her head and again tried to
examine her sister's letter.

" Sir Charles Bellingham his name is; but
she does not describe him at all. I wish
she had : I should have liked to imagine

him to myself—my new brother, as he will be. I suppose he is young and very handsome: Augusta is so beautiful herself."

" Your father says more about him, fortunately," said Mr. Talbot, who had been looking over his son-in-law's epistle. " 'Everything I could wish for in a husband for my daughter—excellent family—good fortune — distinguished position — talents of no mean order—a large proprietor in ——shire, where his ancestral home is situated, &c. &c.' That is all, my dear; I am sorry there is nothing about his age or his looks. Stay, I can give you information on one point in a moment: fetch me ' Burke's Baronetage.' There you will see the fullest particulars of his family, age, and everything else."

Marian brought the volume as desired, and very soon was mistress of all the more important points connected with the position of her future brother-in-law: which she proceeded to impart to her grandfather and grandmother, the latter of whom had just entered the room.

"Augusta says her marriage will not be very long delayed, grandmamma; and I am to be one of her bridesmaids. Oh! doesn't it all seem like a dream?" said Marian, enthusiastically, as the letter again fell on her lap, and her sparkling eyes were raised eagerly to the two loving old faces so tenderly gazing on the now delighted girl.

"I am very glad you are so happy, my dear," observed Mrs. Talbot, gently; "but you must remember that the dream so bright and pleasant to you will have a sad awakening for us. Summerton will be a changed home without the little Marian who has so long been its sunshine."

Marian was on the ground by her side in an instant, both arms thrown impulsively round her loved grandmother's waist.

"Dear grandmamma! do you think for a moment that I am going to leave you altogether? Did you ever, for one instant, imagine that? You, who have been mother, grandmother, and sister, and everything to me! No, indeed! The very contrary will be the case—we shall never be separated any more, unless for a very short time, now and then, when it may be unavoidable."

"You are rather paradoxical, my dear," said Mr. Talbot, who had now contrived to master the contents of Sir John de Burgh's letter.

"Am I, grandpapa? Listen to me. Papa wont want to live in Italy now, when Augusta is married, and comes to live in her own home in ——shire, as I suppose she will. He will return to England too, to the Abbey, and I shall come with him. That is not at all paradoxical I am sure, but quite plain and easy to be understood."

"Very much so, my dear, if it falls out as you wish it. But suppose your papa does not mean to return to England. He has lived so long abroad, that an English life may have become distasteful to him. And even if he does return to the Abbey, your being there with him, as you will naturally be, is by no means the same thing as having this little curly-head going in and out of the room all day long. The old walls will miss the glad sunbeam that has lighted them up for so many years;" and old Mr. Talbot's voice was husky and broken as he concluded his sentence.

But Marian's warm clasp was round his neck now, and the old gentleman said more cheerily, as he pulled out his bandana and stealthily wiped his eyes, " Well, well dear, we wont say any more about it; it is rather a shame to damp your new-found happiness with our lamentations. I hope your papa and you will come and take up house at the Abbey, and we shall see you as often as we possibly can. How very like the old times it will seem:" and he glanced mournfully at his wife, who responded only by a silent shake of the head.

And now there remained but to make the preparations for their journey; for from the first it was decided that Marian was to be accompanied to her father's home by both her grandfather and her grandmother.

Her delight and happiness were unbounded; and everything around and before her was tinged with the *couleur de rose* that pervaded her youthful and ardent imagination.

The last evening at Summerton was come: they were to set out very early on the morrow. It had been a fine bright day, and Mrs. Talbot being a good deal occupied with various preparations for the journey, Marian and her grandfather had taken a long walk during the afternoon. Garden, shrubbery, home-farm, and a numerous collection of four-footed favourites, had all in turn received a parting visit; and as the day began to draw to a close, and the sombre hues of evening to creep over each long familiar object, Marian's spirits seemed to flag with the waning light, her bright sallies grew fewer and fewer, till at length she walked so slowly and soberly by her grandfather's side that the old gentleman noticed the absence of her wonted vivacity, and turned round to see what was occasioning the unusual silence of his generally voluble companion.

"What is it, my dear?" he inquired, kindly; "you are wonderfully silent this evening."

"Grandpapa," said Marian, in a sad

tone, "I have a very short time here now, and I am beginning to feel very sorry that I am going away. What kind of feeling is a presentiment, grandpapa?"

"What nonsense are you talking, my dear! What have you to do with presentiments; unless it be to foresee that the next time you come to Summerton your papa and Augusta will be here too, and perhaps somebody else you like even better than them?" And here old Mr. Talbot elevated his eyebrows, and tried to look arch and knowing; though that expression quickly died away when he saw that it did not elicit even the faintest shadow of a smile on the grave face of his young granddaughter. "Think how pleasant it will be, darling, when we have you all here together," continued Mr. Talbot, still striving to withdraw her thoughts from what was evidently a melancholy contemplation; "grandmamma and I will grow quite young again!"

"So long as I have looked forward to this visit to Italy," continued Marian,

partly as if speaking to herself; "and now
when it is close at hand, half my anticipated
pleasure in it seems gone."

"That is the way with much in this uncertain world, my dear," replied her grandfather. "Pleasures viewed at a distance
seem more charming than when they come
to be enjoyed. You are fond of poetry,
and must remember that line,

'Man never is, but always to be blest.'"

"I have been very happy at dear old
Summerton," said Marian, with a wistful
glance round the landscape; "and somehow
I feel as if I were bidding it good-bye.
Perhaps it is just because I am leaving it
with an uncertain future before me."

"No doubt of it, my dear, no doubt of
it. You will laugh at all these foolish little
forebodings of yours when you come back
again; but in the meantime don't speak of
them before your grandmamma, or you will
be upsetting her altogether, and that will
never do on the eve of a journey."

They were at home now, and Marian retreated to her own apartment to change her dress and prepare for dinner.

That meal was not so conversational and merry as was usually the case at Summerton; Mrs. Talbot was a little fatigued with her packing and household duties; Marian looked dreamy and absent; even her grandfather seemed infected by her depression, and spoke only when necessary; the old butler and his attendant satellite moved soberly and cautiously, and felt overpowered when the dishes once or twice accidentally rattled; in fact, as that ancient domestic stated afterwards in the servants' hall, "it was the silentest and gloomiest meal as ever he had waited on:" while at a still later period, when he repeated that sentiment, he added with a solemn and sorrowful shake of the head, "Coming events cast their shadows before."

They separated soon that night, for they were to make an early start on the morrow.

Marian speedily dismissed her maid, and

seated herself to engage in the reading and meditation without which she. never closed her day. Her devotions ended, she was about to retire to rest, when, having extinguished her light, she was struck by the wonderful brilliancy of the moonbeams as they shone through the drawn blinds.

Approaching the window, she drew the curtain aside, and stood for a few moments riveted by the calm and exquisite beauty of the scene before her. Next the house was a smoothly-shaven lawn studded with flower-beds; just beyond it a small lake, or rather pond, fringed by a border of graceful shrubs, and shaded by one or two noble horse-chestnuts, that threw their dusky reflections on the glassy surface of the water. A broad gravel path wound round lawn and silent pond; a sunk fence bounded it on the further side, beyond which lay rich park-like meadows, studded with groups of forest trees, beneath some of which lay sleeping cattle, hushed and immovable, their dark forms barely to be distinguished from the thick shadow cast by the closely united though still leafless branches.

Marian leant against the window-frame, drinking in the exquisite loveliness of the scene before her; and as she gazed, that inexplicable feeling of depression returned against which she had been struggling all the afternoon and evening.

"My own dear home! am I indeed bidding you farewell for ever?" she softly murmured to herself, as she recognised the peculiar sensation that had before overpowered her. "Strange that I should feel so sad when it seems that every dream of my childhood and youth is on the point of being so joyfully realized. Is it a mysterious foreshadowing of evil and sorrow in the unknown future; or is it merely that while we remain on earth our fairest hopes must ever be dashed by the contemplation of possible disappointment? Alas! alas! only the future can tell me that dread and hidden secret."

CHAPTER VIII.

ARRIVAL IN ROME.

FIVE o'clock in the afternoon of the day in which the English travellers are expected. The journey has been leisurely taken, for neither Mr. Talbot nor his wife was accustomed to travelling; and it seemed to them a very serious matter to set out for a point so distant as Rome, more especially considering their age and stay-at-home habits. Nevertheless they had enjoyed themselves greatly; and as for Marian, she had cast every gloomy anticipation behind her on crossing the Channel, and had entered with the keenest zest of novelty and youthful exhilaration into all the strange and animated scenes through which they had passed. Who can describe her enthusiasm at the first sight of Rome! The Eternal City! The Mistress of the World!

It was before the days of the railway, which now makes the journey from Civita Vecchia an affair of three hours at most; and the travellers had still a longish drive before them after the first glimpse of the vast dome and the buildings that showed white on the hill-side beyond the brown Campagna.

At last they reached the gate, and after a brief detention their carriage rattled on over the wretched pavement of Rome.

The daylight waned as they drove on past the colonnades of St. Peter's, and heard a bell somewhere in the precincts of the church knelling forth the hour; low, deep, reverberating, " swinging slow with solemn roar;" and saw the stately pillars standing tall and pale in the fading light around the noble court which they enclose, and then the mass of St. Angelo, and the statues on the bridge.

. After a while the carriage turned a sharp corner out of a dull dark street, and entered the brighter and busier Corso.

A minute or two more and it stopped

before the deep entrance of the Palazzo R——, the present residence of Sir John de Burgh. In the stately *salon* were seated Sir John and Augusta. Uncertain of the precise hour when the travellers might arrive, they had remained at home during the afternoon, and denied themselves to all visitors with the exception of Sir Charles Bellingham, who now might naturally rank as one of the family. He was with them now, sitting close by his fair *fiancée*, with whom he was conversing in a low tone, not to disturb Sir John in his perusal of some rather ponderous looking volume. In his pretended perusal we should say, for Sir John was not reading, though his hands held the book towards him, and his eyes were apparently bent on its open pages. Beneath that calm and unmoved exterior, his heart was beating thick and fast at the thoughts of the anticipated meeting.

Presently he laid the book down and listened. " I think I hear them now," he said. The next moment his words were confirmed by the violent ringing of a bell.

Sir John rose to his feet with an effort, at the same time turning very pale.

"Let us go down and meet them," he observed, making a sign to Augusta to accompany him.

She rose in her dark stately beauty, and prepared to descend the staircase with her father and her lover. It was fully lighted up, and the first glance showed that the travellers were just entering the house.

Mr. and Mrs. Talbot were in the foreground, and with them Sir John was presently shaking hands very cordially, though there was a nervous shrinking in the manner in which he avoided looking beyond them that evinced his dread of what was still to be encountered. For a little figure stood quiet and trembling in the shade behind, gazing with wistful eyes on the stately form that she knew to be her father's, but not daring to claim acknowledgment until it should be his pleasure to search for and address her. And he saw her and knew that it was his long-forsaken child; but a feeling of hesitation and fear made him even now strive to postpone the moment of recognition till it was inevitably forced on him.

Still retaining his hold of Mrs. Talbot's hand, he turned round to introduce Augusta, who had remained slightly aloof, but who now came gracefully forward and united her greeting to her father's, as she submitted to, rather than reciprocated, the warm embrace bestowed on her by both her grand-parents.

"But where is my little girl?" said Mr. Talbot, hastily looking round, and then drawing forward the little form so slight and shrinking. "Here is your little Marian, Sir John; whose sole thought, day and night, since she received your letter, has been the joy of this meeting."

The lamplight fell brightly on the sweet young face, on the shining golden tresses, on the soft blue eyes so lovingly raised to his. Sir John gave but one glance, then clasping his hands on his forehead, he uttered a deep groan that seemed to rend his very heart; and staggering against the marble balustrade on which he leant heavily for support, he exclaimed, hoarsely, "Take her away—for God's sake take her away—it will kill me to look on her again!"

All present were overwhelmed with amazement and horror, and for a moment, no one spoke or moved; till Marian, breaking away from her grandfather's detaining grasp, sprang quickly forward and threw herself impetuously at her father's feet.

"Papa! papa!" she cried, in agony, as with blanched features and streaming eyes, she seized one of his hands and covered it with convulsive kisses; "papa! papa! you will never send me away from you again! I could not bear it; indeed, indeed I could not! Oh! look at me, papa, and say you will keep me with you, that you will let me stay with you and be your child. Oh! try and love me, papa, just a very, very little; for I love you so dearly—oh! so very dearly!"

At the first sound of her voice a strong shudder had passed over Sir John de Burgh, and he made an effort to withdraw the hand so firmly clasped by his kneeling daughter. But she held it fast as she poured forth her agonized entreaties; and soon they perceived by the working of his countenance that her pitiful appeal was not addressed to an unlistening ear.

From sheer exhaustion poor little Marian ceased speaking, though her slight form was still shaken by convulsive sobs. There was a moment of silence, which no one ventured to break; though more than one heart present beat almost to bursting with sick anxiety for what was to follow. Another instant and Sir John raised his bent head, and revealed every feature in his face white and stern with suppressed emotion.

Marian looked up too, and for a few never-to-be-forgotten moments father and daughter gazed into each other's eyes, and Sir John seemed, as it were, to drink in every line and lineament of that fair young countenance, which was to him as a vision of one, that when last he looked on it, was lying pure and pale, shrouded in the cerements and trappings of the grave.

Suddenly he leant forward and half opened his arms. Marian sprang into them and nestled closely against his heart; while her father held her fondly to him, kissing over and over again the golden curls that floated over his shoulder, and murmuring softly to himself as he did so, "My Marian! my Marian! Can the grave give up its dead? My child—my own little Marian—you shall never leave me—never—never!"

A sob of irrepressible relief burst from Mrs. Talbot, while her husband wiped the unbidden moisture from his eyes. Sir Charles Bellingham was an interested and not an unmoved spectator; one eye alone remained undimmed of all that gazed upon this scene; one heart only was utterly untouched by a feeling of tenderness or sympathy for the father and daughter so long and strangely parted, and now so closely and lovingly united.

Augusta de Burgh stood calm and silent, no unobservant beholder of what was passing, though by no word or sign did she

betray that it in any way particularly concerned her.

One of the large hall lamps shone just
above her head; but it was not its light
that cast on her rigid countenance that
deep shadow of gloom which seemed to
alter and distort each beautiful feature till
the very lines of her face looked changed,
and an expression gleamed from them
which, had any one been watching her,
might have reminded him of the ancient
legend of the fabled Medusa.

She had listened with unthrobbing pulse
to the piteous appeal of her weeping sister;
the sweet young face so lovely in its
sorrow, the soft blue eyes fast streaming
with tears had touched no tender chord
in her own nature, nay, rather they had
steeled her heart almost into a feeling of
repugnance to the fair and innocent girl
who pleaded so anxiously for the love and
protection of her own father.

When the crisis was past, and Sir John
still clasped the now rejoicing Marian in
his arms, the shadow that clouded the

countenance of his elder daughter became
even darker and deeper in its intensity,
and a cold light glittered in her eyes that
told of stormy passions within, subdued,
but not conquered, by the force of an in-
domitable will.

She still maintained the perfect calmness
of her outward bearing, and gazed with
apparent composure on the *tableau* presented by her father and sister; but Sir
Charles Bellingham chancing to raise his
eyes to her face, was arrested by the concentrated fixedness of her expression, while
an indescribable something in her air and
manner gave him an unpleasant feeling of
discomfort, and silenced the remark he was
on the point of uttering.

Augusta perceived his embarrassment,
and the cause of it; it recalled her to her
ordinary presence of mind, and she turned
smilingly towards him, and endeavoured
to efface the impression she saw he had
received by the more than usual gracious-
ness of her bearing.

But the impression still remained, and

could not be so easily destroyed. More than once that evening Sir Charles found himself recalling it and wondering at it. His final vision of Augusta that night represented her with that gloomy aspect and deadly stare; while the companion picture that rose to his sight was a slight drooping figure, with long fair ringlets and tear-bedewed cheeks, the little English sister of his dark and stately ladye love.

But we are digressing.

The first excitement over, it became necessary that the ordinary routine of life should recover its ascendancy. No one seemed inclined to assume the initiative; till Augusta, stepping forward to the place where her father still stood supporting Marian, said, in a voice carefully toned to sympathy, but which had yet a strange ring in it, " Come, papa; you have had more than your fair share of my sister; it is my turn to welcome her now." She took Marian's hand in hers as she spoke, and the young girl yielded to the slight compulsion, and raised herself from her resting-place on her father's shoulder. Tearfully she lifted her blue eyes to her sister's; and had but one loving glance re-assured her, she would have flung her arms fondly round that dear sister's neck, and sobbed out her joy at seeing her. But the heart has an instinct in those matters beyond the mere power of reasoning; and in those beautiful dark eyes of Augusta's poor Marian read no answering gladness at the meeting, but an expression all new and strange to her, which had nevertheless the effect of checking the impulsive ardour of her greeting. Marian felt chilled, she could not tell why, for Augusta's manner seemed all that could be desired; the little girl only knew that she was disappointed without being exactly able to describe her reason for being so.

"Perhaps it must always be so," was her meek reflection afterwards. "So many things in this world seem brighter at a distance than they do when near. And Augusta! so beautiful and so much made of as she has always been, how could I have expected her to feel the same longing to meet me that I have had to meet her? I was unreasonable in supposing such a thing possible." Poor little humble-minded Marian!

A diversion had now been skilfully effected: fresh cordial greetings took place. Sir Charles Bellingham was introduced to his future relatives, and the whole party adjourned to the *salon*.

But Sir John de Burgh was still silent and preoccupied; he joined but little in the conversation, and gazed often and mournfully on the face of his younger daughter; while the deep sighs that every now and then burst from him clearly betokened the melancholy reminiscences which had been awakened by the sight of her form and features.

He had led her upstairs himself and placed her on a sofa beside him: it seemed as if he now could not have enough of his fair young daughter so long and so cruelly neglected.

Mr. and Mrs. Talbot witnessed his behaviour with the keenest satisfaction; while Marian herself felt that her delight and gratitude at his evident interest and affection more than counterbalanced her regret at the unmistakeable indifference of her sister.

It would be difficult to analyse the condition of mind in which Augusta found herself when, the necessary attention to her guests being over, she left them to rest until dinner-time, and betook herself to the silence and solitude of her own apartment. Fierce jealousy was raging in her heart; jealousy of that innocent young girl so long deserted and forsaken, but who had at once and unexpectedly taken up a position and assumed an importance in her father's consideration which Augusta felt, with keen mortification, had never been accorded to her. She felt as if a rival had entered the lists, a rival potent and dangerous; and it was with bitter humiliation that Augusta acknowledged to herself that every weapon in her armoury must be got ready to enable her to cope with this unlooked-for and powerful assailant.

Tearful and travel-marked as she was, Augusta had been compelled to admit the exceeding loveliness of her sister; and feeling certain from all she had heard, as well as from a miniature in Sir John's possession, that in features and person she perfectly resembled her long-lamented mother, Miss de Burgh arrived very speedily at the conclusion that it would require more than ordinary skill and management if she desired to prevent this interloper, as she now considered her, from obtaining an undue and undesirable influence over her father.

Carefully reflecting upon all this, Augusta rang for her maid, and attiring herself for the evening, she again descended to the *salon*, and prepared to resume her duties as hostess.

Presently her sister entered the room, following in the wake of Mr. and Mrs. Talbot.

If she had seemed so charming before in her plain dark travelling garments, how much more lovely did she look now in a soft white robe of Indian muslin, a few coral ornaments, formerly sent home to her by Augusta, her sole attempt at decoration. She generally permitted her beautiful fair hair to flow loosely round her shoulders in the evening; just so her mother had been in the habit of wearing it, and it pleased her grandfather that she should resemble her in this respect as in so many others.

Therefore, to Sir John de Burgh it seemed as though the long years intervening were but as a dream, and that his long-lost wife again stood before him in all the fulness of the fresh and innocent beauty he had never ceased to remember.

It was easy to see of what he was thinking when his younger daughter entered the room; for he advanced to meet her, and placing one arm fondly on her shoulder he drew her towards him, and sighing deeply as his eye took in each well-remembered point of likeness, he gently stooped and imprinted a tender fatherly kiss on the pure white forehead that was timidly raised to meet his embrace. Augusta· observed all, and there was a feeling as of a sudden spasm at her heart; but she rigidly compressed her lips to restrain all outward semblance of emotion: and if her cheek were a trifle paler and her countenance rather sterner than ordinary, no one was noticing her at the moment, or would have attached any particular significance to it if they had been.

After dinner they adjourned to the *salon;* and very speedily Augusta was called upon to give her English relations an opportunity of judging for themselves of the magnificent voice, the fame of which had so often reached their ears.

She complied at once, for all mock modesty was foreign to her nature.

"I rarely sing anything but Italian music," she observed to her grandfather, who was sitting near the piano; "and I fear you will not care for it so much as for an English song."

" Ballads are certainly what I prefer,"

replied Mr. Talbot; "I understand them better, and many of them have old associations for me: but a good thing can never come amiss, and a very good thing your voice must be, if all is true that I have heard about it."

Augusta smiled, and proceeded to sing a lovely aria of Mozart's. It was a very well known one, and Mr. Talbot had often heard it in his younger days at the Opera, so it gratified him to listen again to the once familiar melody. She sang it exquisitely, and Marian sat by completely entranced by the beauty of the performance.

"Oh! how delicious!" she exclaimed, with unaffected enthusiasm, when her sister concluded. "Please, Augusta, do give us another."

"I second that request," said Mr. Talbot. "I enjoy that music thoroughly; so I am not entirely a Vandal, my dear. Perhaps I may acquire a taste for Italian music during my residence here."

"Quite possible," replied Augusta, as she sat down and sang something else which gave them equal gratification. "Now, Marian," she continued, as she laid aside the music-book, "I am sure you sing, and it is your turn now."

Poor Marian coloured and looked distressed; she, too, was accustomed to sing as soon as she was requested, but she felt completely overwhelmed with nervousness and timidity now.

"I see we are terribly overcome," observed Mr. Talbot, kindly, as he caught his granddaughter's appealing glance; "but there is no need to be so very much alarmed, my dear. You have a very sweet little pipe of your own, and there are no severe judges here. One of your pretty little ballads will contrast very nicely with Augusta's more elaborate style."

Shyly and shrinkingly poor Marian obeyed, and seated herself at the piano.

She felt still more unnerved when her father, who had been sitting at some little distance and conversing in an undertone with Mrs. Talbot, at the first sound of her voice rose, hesitated for a moment, and then quitting his seat, slowly approached the instrument.

For a moment or two she was doubtful whether she could possibly go on; then she called to remembrance that it was her duty, as it would ever be her pleasure, to do all that lay in her power to afford him gratification: the thought of this gave her courage, and the next instant her sweet bird-like tones rang clearly through the room as she sang one of those touching old English ballads that will retain their place in the hearts of the people as long as their language lasts.

Sir John's eyes filled with tears as he listened; the song had been a favourite with his dead wife, and very often she had sung it at his request. Just such a sweet limpid voice was hers—such a voice as it is pleasant to hear in the dreamy twilight hour, before the candles are brought in, and when the flickering firelight throws weird shadows on the wall.

Marian ceased, and her father thanked her cordially, then he asked her for another and another; and when at last she quitted the piano, he took her in his arms for a moment and kissed her tenderly.

"God bless you, my child!" he said, in a low tone of deep emotion. "Looking at you and listening to you brings back feelings that I thought were for ever buried in the grave." And Augusta heard him, and the iron seemed to enter into her soul.

CHAPTER IX.

FIRST IMPRESSIONS.

When he quitted the abode of his fair *fiancée* Sir Charles Bellingham returned home, and found his mother already expecting him.

" The travellers have arrived I suppose ?" said Lady Agnes, as he entered the room where she was sitting.

" Yes," replied her son; " they made their appearance just before I left."

" Well! and what of the little English beauty, the invisible princess? Is she so very charming as has been represented?" And Lady Agnes suspended operations on her knitting, and smilingly awaited her son's reply.

" She is excessively pretty, there is no doubt of that," said Sir Charles; " a perfect little Queen Mab or Titania, a most wonderful contrast to Augusta. But as far as I could judge, she seemed a mere child. The idea of anybody wanting to marry her is simply preposterous."

"She is about seventeen," remarked his mother; "I think Augusta said that was her age. So she is not quite such a child."

"She looks fifteen at most," said Sir Charles; "a creature that should be playing with her doll instead of receiving proposals of marriage. Not but that she is pretty enough to have dozens of them; a regular little fairy with her blue eyes and her golden curls. It was the most charming picture possible, to see her lying in her father's arms, with her fair hair streaming over his shoulder:" and the young man proceeded to describe Sir John's behaviour on the arrival of his younger daughter.

"Poor little thing!" said Lady Agnes, wiping her eyes as she listened; "it must have been a very trying scene for all concerned, but I am glad that all seems established on a proper footing now. How did

Augusta act on the occasion? I hope she was very tender to the poor child?"

Sir Charles rather hesitated, for it was difficult to describe Miss de Burgh's conduct, though it had certainly not been tender; and the uncomfortable feeling once more recurred to his mind that had arisen there when first he observed that strange and disagreeable expression on the fair countenance of his betrothed bride.

"Oh! well, Augusta had nothing very particular to do," he remarked at length. "In fact, nobody had much to do except Sir John and Marian. When they had got over their little excitement, every one became rational and commonplace directly." Lady Agnes heard and understood; but by no sign did she show that such was the case.

She quietly continued her conversation with her son; and when she had heard all she wished to know, she merely declared that at an early hour on the following day she should take the opportunity of calling on Mrs. Talbot and her granddaughter, as she was naturally anxious to form the acquaintance of people so soon to be nearly connected with her family.

Accordingly, in the course of the next forenoon, Lady Agnes Bellingham, accompanied by her son, presented herself for admittance at Sir John de Burgh's palazzo in the Corso. They were ushered into the large *salon*, which at that moment was tenanted only by Mr. and Mrs. Talbot and Marian.

The old gentleman was studying an English newspaper; Mrs. Talbot was winding a skein of worsted, which her young grand-daughter, seated on a low stool at her feet, was holding on her extended hands. It was a pretty picture, home-like and English looking in that foreign city; and Lady Agnes felt a sensation of pleasure as she gazed on the happy group.

Both ladies rose immediately on her entrance, and very cordial greetings were interchanged; the whole party presently falling into a thoroughly easy and agreeable conversation, which was not at all inter-

rupted by the arrival of Sir John de Burgh
and his elder daughter.

Marian formed the strangest possible contrast to Augusta, who took a chair so placed,
that both the sisters were almost in a line.
The brilliant beauty of the elder, enhanced
by every art and attraction of the most
exquisite *toilette*, seemed at the first glance to
cast into the shade the little figure in sober
morning dress, only relieved by a snowy
linen collar and cuffs, and the gold locket
that hung from her neck containing a tress
of her mother's hair. But the more Lady
Agnes gazed on the innocent face of the
younger Miss de Burgh, the more strongly
she felt her heart drawn towards her.
Lovely as she undeniably was, her beauty
was but a slight part of the charm that
attracted so many hearts: her winning
manner and artless, childlike disposition
were gifts far more potent and irresistible.
Lady Agnes watched her with kindly attention, and when Sir John de Burgh
made an observation, she perceived that
Marian was always deeply interested in

whatever he said; her eyes sparkled and the soft colour mantled in her cheek; clearly he was an object of the warmest solicitude to her, and this evidence of her love for the father who had so cruelly neglected her, endeared her still more to the kind heart that was already so strongly attracted to her.

She was still engaged in studying Marian, when Sir John chanced to notice the direction of her glance.

"Ah! Lady Agnes," he remarked, "I wish especially to bespeak your friendship for my younger daughter. I must have you better acquainted; Marian, my dear, come here."

She rose at once at his summons, and crossing over to where he was, she took the seat he placed for her between Lady Agnes and himself. "This is my little English rosebud," he said, laying his hand softly on her head and twisting one golden tendril gently in his fingers. "She is her mother's very image, Lady Agnes; I can scarcely say whether it gives me most pleasure or pain to have her with me." But his looks were expressive only of pleasure and love, though there was a mournful tenderness in his gaze.

"I am sure she will be nothing but a joy and a comfort to you, Sir John," replied her ladyship; "and when you are deprived of Augusta this young lady will be the very person to supply her place."

"I have but a small claim on her affection," said Sir John, sadly; "I have very sorely neglected my duty as a father hitherto, though I hope to do my best to atone for it now."

"Do not talk so, papa," whispered Marian, gently, her eyes filling with tears and her colour deepening as she spoke; "I love you very, very dearly; and I know the reason why you never sent for me here."

There was a moment's silence, and Mr. Talbot appealed to his son-in-law to confirm some observation he had just made. Sir John joined in the discussion, and Lady Agnes continued her conversation with Marian.

"How do you think you shall like Italy, my dear? As well as England?"

"Oh! no," replied Marian, eagerly; "no place can ever be to me like England. It has always been my home."

"But Italy will probably be your home now; for some time at least."

"Only for a time, I hope," said Marian. "Papa will surely return to England soon—after Augusta is married, I hope."

"I see you like England best," continued Lady Agnes, smiling. "But when you know a little more of this charming country, I venture to pronounce that you will become very fond of it. I am a thoroughbred John Bull, and yet I like Italy exceedingly."

"But not so well as England?" said Marian, inquiringly.

"Certainly not: we are quite of one mind there. Summerton is a very pretty place, I believe? I have been in your county, in another part of it."

"Oh! it is very pretty," replied Marian, warmly: "such a dear old place, a regular English manor-house. I had so many things to make me fond of it.   I have been there ever since I was a child, and knew every corner of it.   I had my garden—and lots of pets," she continued, with a merry laugh and bright blush; "and all the old people and children about the place were especial cronies of mine.   I should be very, very sorry if I thought I was not to return to Summerton."   She glanced to where her grandfather and grandmother were sitting, and her soft lip quivered and large tears came into the eager blue eyes.

"I did not mean that for a moment, my dear," said Lady Agnes, kindly.   "I hope you will very often revisit Summerton: what I meant was that in all human probability it will never again be your home. That will naturally be with your father now; for the present at any rate."

"And a very short time that will be, if English gentlemen see with my eyes," was her ladyship's inward comment as she finished speaking.

Shortly afterwards she rose to take leave;

Sir Charles, however, remaining behind to escort his *fiancée* in her forenoon ride.

" Ah! dear," was the meditation of Lady Agnes, as her carriage drove off, " I suppose it is for our good that the very desire and longing of our hearts is so often withheld from us. That is the very sweetest girl I ever saw in my life!"

Other visitors were very speedily announced; " Mrs. Greville and Miss Crewe." Augusta had withdrawn to prepare for riding: Sir John de Burgh and Sir Charles Bellingham had gone to issue directions respecting the horses. Therefore it happened that Mrs. Greville devoted herself to the old couple, while Emily seated herself in the immediate vicinity of Marian, and addressed herself to the task of discovering what kind of mental qualifications existed behind what she was afterwards pleased to term " the most enchanting little face she had ever set·her eyes on."

Under the perfect frankness and genuine goodnature of her manner Marian presently found all her reserve and shyness thawing away; indeed, in a very short time she was laughing heartily at some of Miss Crewe's observations. A character such as Emily was something new and strange to the homebred English girl, accustomed to the quiet and orthodox society usually to be found in country neighbourhoods, where anything so startling as the fair Irishwoman would have been regarded as rather an appalling and dangerous specimen of the genus feminine.

"I see you are horribly shy," said Emily, with perfect candour. "Most English girls are: but you will soon lose it here. Nothing like the Continent for getting rid of our insular rust."

"Were you ever shy?" inquired Marian, anxiously.

"Never, my dear; don't know the meaning of the word, experimentally at least. I come of that much maligned race the Irish; we are not supposed to be especially gifted with modesty, you know. But I want you to tell me how you think you shall like Italy and things in general. We have all been on the *qui vive* for your arrival here. You have been like a little enchanted princess shut up in a demon-guarded castle."

"Indeed, I have not," replied Marian, colouring. "I have always lived with the very kindest of grand-parents : no person ever had a happier home than I have had."

"A thousand pardons, my dear!" said Emily, warmly. "I did not mean that for a moment. Only we all knew the fact of your existence; and from what we had heard," and she smiled, archly, "we all wanted very much to see you."

"And I think now that some people have seen you, they will be wishing to pack you up and send you back again directly," thought Miss Crewe to herself, though she was wiser than to say it aloud. "I need not ask if you have seen your future brother-in-law?" she added.

"Oh! yes, I have seen him twice; and I am sure I shall like him exceedingly. He is very handsome and pleasant-looking; and

what a beautiful old lady his mother is! I
have quite lost my heart to her already, she
spoke to me so very kindly."

"Ah! you are just the girl to suit her,"
thought Emily.

"Lady Agnes is charming," was her
answer to Marian; "to my mind she is the
most perfect picture of an old English
gentlewoman that I ever saw: such calm
repose of manner and dignified simplicity
of style."

"Exactly," replied Marian, warmly; "I
think my sister fortunate in the prospect
of such a delightful mother-in-law. I hope
she will live with them after they are married."

"Oh! surely not," said Miss Crewe, in a
surprised tone : "that would never answer
at all."

"Why not?" asked Marian, simply;
"Lady Agnes has always lived with her
son."

"Yes, while he was a bachelor," replied
Emily, smiling. "When he is a married
man she will prefer a home of her own."

" Will she?" remarked Marian, as if the idea were a new one to her. " I don't see why they should not all live together: I know I should wish it so were I in Augusta's place."

" But you see you are different from Miss de Burgh," said Emily, kindly, thinking how true this observation was. " You have never been at the head of a household, as your sister has. Little difficulties would be constantly arising. Two mistresses are an awkward matter in the same house."

" I did not think of that," replied Marian; " well, perhaps it might be the case."

Their conversation continued for some time, Miss Crewe becoming more and more struck with Marian's gentle purity and sweetness, until something of respect and reverence was mingled with her fast growing interest in the younger Miss de Burgh. They were presently interrupted by the entrance of Augusta, her father, and her lover, all three prepared for their ride; and Miss Crewe and her sister shortly afterwards took leave.

"Well, what do you think of the new arrivals, or rather of the new Miss de Burgh?" demanded Mrs. Greville of Emily as they traversed the Corso on their return homewards.

"What do I think of her!" she replied, in an excited tone; "oh! Norah! I feel as if I could tear my hair and gnash my teeth this very minute in the open street."

"My dear Emily! whatever is the mat·ter?" said Mrs. Greville, looking wonderingly round.

"Oh! you obtuse old thing!" exclaimed Emily, laughing; "don't you take my meaning at all? Don't you see, as plain as a pike-staff (whatever that figure of speech may signify), that this identical little girl was made, created, cut and dried, for one particular purpose?"

"What purpose?" asked Mrs. Greville, opening her eyes. "Really, Emily, to hear you talk sometimes, people would think you were half-crazy."

"And so I am at this present moment," retorted Miss Crewe, in a voice of half-amusement, half-annoyance; "quite crazy with vexation to think of what might have been if only things would have fallen out as one wished. Why! don't you see that this little girl from England, Marian de Burgh, exactly, in every single jot and tittle, fulfils my idea of the wife I always told you I should have selected for Sir Charles Bellingham?"

"Oh! that is your meaning, is it?" said Mrs. Greville, looking much relieved. "Why could not you have said so at once without all this preamble! She is very pretty, certainly; but not more so than her sister."

"It is not her beauty," replied Miss Crewe; "I daresay many people would say Miss de Burgh was far handsomer; it is the charm of every look, of every word she utters—the unmistakable sweetness of her disposition and goodness of her heart—in short, she was made for Sir Charles, and is the exact style of daughter-in-law Lady Agnes would have chosen."

"Men don't usually marry to please their mothers," retorted Norah. "Sir Charles has probably chosen to please himself."

"Umph?" said Miss Crewe, rather shortly. She had a theory of her own on this head; but she had never mentioned it to her sister or to anyone else. "Of course I am only speaking of what might have been," she continued, after a few moments' pause; "no good whatever thinking of such matters now. Sir Charles has chosen a bride for himself, and a very beautiful and stately one without doubt; but what a dear little Lady Bellingham this pretty Marian would have made: looking after her flower-garden, and her schools, and her poor people, as she has been accustomed to do all her life; adoring her husband, and giving the care and affection of a daughter to Lady Agnes—really, when one thinks of all they have lost, I feel as if it would be a perfectly allowable proceeding to stop the banns at the very church door, and declare that a just and lawful impediment exists in the person of a far more suitable wife for the bridegroom."

"My dear Emily, I hope you won't talk all this nonsense to anyone but me," said Mrs. Greville seriously; "you might do a great deal of harm by it."

"Most potent, wise, and reverend Norah," replied the fair Emily with mock solemnity, "do you take me to be a fool? or can you name any particular instance in which I have acted the part of a mischief-maker, or a busy-body? Because if you do, state the occasion."

"I did not mean that, Emily; but you do rattle on so tremendously."

"That may be, sister mine; but all things have their limits, and so has my nonsense. I shall not overstep the bounds of discretion."

"Now, Emily, you know I did not intend to hurt your feelings. Don't be cross with me; there's a darling."

CHAPTER X.

SINCE that eventful evening when they parted on the moonlit terrace, Miss de Burgh had neither seen nor heard anything of Count Salvi. He quitted Rome directly afterwards, and no one appeared to be aware of his whereabouts.

Some rumours had gone abroad of a misunderstanding between him and Miss de Burgh: either she had rejected him or they had quarrelled—something at least was understood to be the matter, though no one dared for one moment have ventured on the liberty of asking that young lady a question on the subject; and for some weeks Count Salvi's name had not even been mentioned in her hearing.

She was therefore not a little surprised, a

few mornings later, on descending from her carriage and entering a well-known library, to find Count Salvi standing in the shop, glancing over some newly-arrived books. He raised his hat and saluted her courteously, but gravely; and Miss de Burgh, for once in her life taken quite aback, felt herself reduced to the necessity of returning his bow, unless she preferred attracting an unpleasant amount of observation from various persons scattered about the library.

A very cold and distant bow it was however; not such a one as to encourage the recipient to address her: nevertheless, Count Salvi dared the haughty stare of those unflinching eyes, and followed Miss de Burgh into the remote corner where she affected to be absorbed in her contemplation of the volume she held in her hand.

"Miss De Burgh, hear me; but for one moment permit me to speak to you."

"Leave me, Count Salvi," replied Augusta, without raising her eyes. "I wish to hold no communication with you."

"One moment—just one moment," he

pleaded, "and then, if you bid me, I will leave you for ever."

"I desire you to go now," said Augusta icily, at the same time looking him full in the face.

He shrank not; his gaze was as intrepid as her own. "*Tu me lo pagherai!*" was his bitter inward exclamation, as he watched her cruel beauty and scornful bearing; "some day or other I may be able to repay you all this, fair lady; and small pity will I show you then!"

But he only said with quiet firmness, "I have offended you, Miss de Burgh; I own it, and I am here now to plead for forgiveness. Surely I am right in supposing that your nature is too generous to harbour resentment against the poor wretch whom your beauty nearly maddened. In one fatal moment I forgot myself, and I spoke words then that I have repented ever since, and that I shall repent to the latest hour of my existence. Will you not forgive me now?"

Arrested, in spite of herself, by the quiet

force of his manner, Augusta had heard his explanation to the end.

"I may forgive you, Count Salvi," she replied with perfect calmness, "but I can never forget the words you spoke to me that night. After what then passed between us we can never again be friends: therefore in future it will be better that we do not meet."

"That must be as you decide," he said, with humble deprecation; "but I would still say a few words more. You are now prosperous and happy; the chosen bride of one whom, alas! I know too well how dearly you love. In the bright sunshine of love and happiness, you will not heed the one faint shadow that at a distance may flit across your path; seek not to drive me utterly from your presence; it will be death to me if you do. Hearing, as I did, even in absence, all that had befallen you, I struggled to tear my hopeless passion from my heart. It mattered not if all life died within me, so that all love died too. The proof that I have succeeded is that I am here, feeling all that I have done, knowing all that I do.   You will not bid me begone now; you will let me see you sometimes. We were good friends once; may those old happy days never return?"

In spite of every precaution on the part of Count Salvi, he had not been entirely successful in toning down his voice to the measured accents of ordinary friendly converse.   One or two rather curious glances had been cast in their direction; Augusta observed this, and felt that the interview had lasted long enough.

" I must go now," she said, moving a step forwards as she spoke; " I shall think over what you have said; I cannot decide at present."

He knew her too well to urge her further; and bowing deeply, he accompanied her through the shop, and handed her into the carriage, which was in waiting.   She could not refuse his proffered assistance, though she accepted it most reluctantly; and as she sank back among the cushions she bent her head very coldly in return for the count's prolonged obeisance, and the expression that gleamed from her half-closed eyes was very much the reverse of agreeable.

"Vittoria! vittoria!" muttered the Italian, as he watched the carriage turn the corner before quitting his respectful attitude, "I have gained my point; she can never retract now. I have publicly been seen to hand her into her carriage. It was scarcely so hard a matter either as I had anticipated; these women are terrible fools if one can only find their soft side; not that there is much softness, or much of the woman either for that matter about her; she is a fiend, or I am very much mistaken. Had she lived about a century ago, I should not like to have been the obstacle that stood in her way! It would have been, hey! presto! gone! Some day she and I may yet have a little account to settle. I am not one to forget injuries any more than herself; and I have by no means forgotten some civil observations she was kind enough to address to me that memorable night when she must have trapped that simple Englishman into proposing for her. He care for her! not an iota, I know that very well; but I own I should like to know how she managed it. There was not much appearance of such a conclusion when we saw that pretty tableau through the window!"

When Augusta came down just before dinner a day or two afterwards, she was met by her father with the not particularly agreeable information that he had encountered their old friend Count Salvi in the street that afternoon, and had invited him to dine with them that evening.

"He did not seem quite willing to accept my invitation at first," continued Sir John, utterly unconscious of the lowering cloud on his daughter's brow; "some scruples about Lent, I suppose, or something of that kind. However, I told him he should do here entirely as he liked, so it ended in his promising to come."

"Very well, papa," said Augusta quietly.

Count Salvi came; there were several other guests, and Miss de Burgh received them all with her usual composed, dignified manner. She just touched the count's hand on his entrance, and he, too prudent to press the matter further at that time, retired into the background, and employed himself in scrutinizing all that went on around him.

"Ah! that is the little English sister," he mentally observed; "per Bacco! but she is a beauty! I marvel much that the reigning monarch tolerates a rival so near the throne. Ah! there is Madame de Mérincourt! *Je suis enchanté de vous voir, madame!* it is an age since we have met."

"Then, will you improve the occasion, Count, by taking charge of Madame de Mérincourt during dinner?" said Sir John de Burgh blandly, as he marshalled his various guests in their respective order.

Nothing could have suited the Count better than having the lively little French-woman as his companion; for he knew that from her he should hear everything he wished to know of the movements of the de Burgh family-circle.

"*Ma foi!* but it was the marvel of every-one," she exclaimed, in reply to some leading question relative to the engagement of Sir

Charles Bellingham and Augusta; "I have not recovered my astonishment at it yet; but after all, *que voulez vous?* It is very suitable in every way."

"And *la belle Irlandaise*, how did she seem to like it?"

"Oh! she never cared for him really. She is gay, *volage*, what in French we call ' *une coquette.*' "

"Coquettes, then, have no hearts, Madame?"

"Ah! *scélérat!* they have too much some-times," and Madame de Mérincourt shrugged her pretty shoulders, gave a languishing roll to her dark eyes, and did all in her power to look sentimental and full of heart.

"But the fair rivals! are they very good friends now?" continued the Count, re-turning to the point.

"Apparently," replied Madame de Mérin-court carelessly. "But what do you think of the new beauty—the younger Miss de Burgh?" she asked. "We have been raving about her in Rome; she is the very last novelty."

"Ah! a pretty little thing, no doubt, but not the style I admire most." Count Salvi here cast a look in the direction of his fair companion, meant to intimate "this is what I prefer."

"But she is excessively charming I assure you," said Madame de Mérincourt, understanding him, and simpering—"indeed I consider her so charming as to be almost dangerous."

"Dangerous! how can she be that?"

"Well, I may be wrong, but I have two or three times noticed that Sir Charles Bellingham seems very much *épris* with this pretty little Marian; and I fancied his fair *fiancée* did not appear quite to like it. Brother and sister they call themselves— the little girl and *le beau futur;* but one does not often see such very devoted attention from a brother to a sister. However, it is no concern of mine; they must look to that for themselves."

"You are right, Madame; one is seldom thanked for interfering in the affairs of other people;" and the count having now arrived at a pretty clear understanding of the subject in which he was interested, permitted their conversation gradually to wander to other topics.

Other guests joined the party in the evening, and they had some music.

The Austrian Ambassadress was a remarkably fine performer on the piano ; she played a sonata of Beethoven's in faultless style, but it was rather long and dreary, and the movement had but little variety in it.   Her rank commanded the silence which might otherwise have been exceptional, for there are people to whom Beethoven's sonatas are very much the reverse of a treat.

Marian sat near the piano, really enjoying the beauty of the music, but sadly distracted by the conduct of Sir Charles Bellingham, who would make grimaces at her expressive of profound weariness, holding an engraving before his face as a precaution while he did so, and taking very good care that the Ambassador was looking another way.

Once or twice her enforced seriousness gave way, and an irresistible smile illumined her features for a moment, to be succeeded by a deep blush and a more tremendous gravity than before.

"I really wonder at you, Marian!—so silly!" said Augusta, as she returned from thanking the fair performer. Marian felt overwhelmed, and never for one moment attempted to justify herself.

"Don't scold her, Augusta; it was all my fault," remarked Sir Charles, laughingly, as he immediately joined the two sisters. "But how could any mortal creature be expected to sit still and do nothing during that endless overture, or whatever you call it? Do let us have something rational now, and rather under an hour, if possible. Sing yourself; and I see you have got that fellow Salvi back again—make him sing too. It's the only thing he is fit for."

"Don't you like Count Salvi?" inquired Marian, as her future brother-in-law pulled forward a chair and seated himself beside her.

"I hate him like poison, my dear; or, as that is rather unrefined language, I cherish a very profound and particular antipathy to him, which I have some reason to flatter myself is cordially returned by the young nobleman in question."

"But he is very intimate here, isn't he?" said Marian. "I have heard he was a great friend of Augusta's; they used to sing together very often."

"Yes, at one time he was constantly here," replied Sir Charles; "one came across him at all sorts of uncomfortable hours, slinking about the house like a tame cat— there *is* something very feline in his style. I used to think he was dangling after your sister, and so I believe he was." Certain recollections here made the young baronet wince a little and become rather red. "And, now I think of it," he continued, speaking more energetically, "see that he does not make himself over to you, Marian; it would be very like him to do so, and I warn you that I wont receive him as my brother-in-law on any account. I must have something very super-excellent for my little sister—not a fellow like that!"

"Charles, you are really most absurd!"

and Marian smiled and blushed very becomingly indeed.

"What is he saying that is so absurd?" Augusta stood behind them, having just arrived in time to hear the conclusion of the little discussion. Neither of them knew exactly what to reply; Sir Charles hesitated, while Marian blushed yet more deeply than before.

"Oh! I beg your pardon; I have no wish whatever to pry into your secrets!" And Augusta was gone, with a very lowering expression on her countenance.

"Augusta! nonsense! It was the merest trifle," exclaimed Sir Charles, endeavouring to arrest her departure; but she paid no heed to him, and in the indignation of the moment, scarcely knowing what she was doing, she advanced towards Count Salvi and begged him to favour them with a song, a request with which, especially as coming from her, he was only too delighted to comply.

The little incident we have related had been observed with the keenest interest by the Count. He had been watching Sir Charles Bellingham's behaviour to the two sisters very narrowly; and it struck him that Madame de Mérincourt's observation as to the good understanding that seemed to exist between the younger Miss de Burgh and her future brother-in-law was by no means irrelevant or undeserved. To one so keenly alive to every expression of human nature as Count Salvi, nothing was more palpably evident than the fact that the young baronet was by no means passionately attached to his betrothed bride. He was proud of her beauty, and liked her, nay, it might be, *loved* her to a certain qualified extent; but his best affections, those ardent feelings that are as the first fruits and joyful offering of a warm and generous disposition, such an attachment, such a love as this, the count saw very clearly was not bestowed upon Augusta de Burgh. Why, then, had he proposed to her? That was the problem that puzzled him.

He resolved to watch and wait; he had a long score to settle with the haughty heiress, who had rejected his proffered love, not with the tender pity of a compassionate woman, but with the bitter loathing of one who spurns the poisonous adder from her path.

He had told her then that his love was as a raging torrent, breaking down every barrier, so that only its desire might be accomplished: she should yet find that equally fierce and unconquerable was his hatred; which, in a disposition like that of Count Salvi, was even more of a master passion, more in accordance with the cool, crafty, merciless nature, that fully grafted with all the worst vices of his countrymen, had yet imbibed nothing that was pure, true, or honourable.

But no sign of all this was to be traced in his smiling countenance now, as bowing a ready compliance with the wish expressed by his fair hostess, he accompanied her towards the piano.

"What shall I sing?" asked the count, striking a few introductory chords. "Have you any choice, Miss de Burgh?"

"None," she replied politely, but distantly, "I leave it entirely to yourself."

He reflected for a moment, and then sang Schubert's "Wanderer" with exquisite taste and feeling. There was a murmur of admiration when he had finished, and a chorus of eager dissent when he rose as if to leave the piano.

"It is most charming," said the Austrian ambassadress graciously; "I do hope we may beg for another."

"You are fond of music, *madame?*" observed Sir John; "then, if we can prevail on the count to sing a duet with my daughter, I venture to say you will be very much gratified. Augusta, my dear, will you and Count Salvi kindly oblige us?"

She had no excuse ready, and before she had time to frame one, Count Salvi had bowed his acquiescence, and was already looking for the volume of Italian duets. It opened at one which they had often sung together; the count placed it on the desk before her, and Augusta felt herself unwillingly compelled to accept the position so publicly forced on her, and occupy the seat from which Count Salvi had just risen.

She felt annoyed and outwitted, and began half mechanically to play the introductory prelude. By a curious coincidence, the piece which had been selected was a quarrel between a betrothed pair, or rather the return of the lover, penitent, and humbly suing for forgiveness.

Count Salvi threw all his voice and energy into his part, and touchingly bewailed his hard fate in having fallen under the ban of his adored one's displeasure.

Beautiful as was the melody, it was rendered still more so by the marvellous singing of the count, who pronounced every word and delivered every note with the taste and feeling of a perfect master of the emotion which he wished to produce.

It thrilled to the hearts of the listeners. Augusta herself, steeled by her pride and aversion against any inclination to tenderness, was irresistibly penetrated by the pathos that breathed from every syllable; and the inexplicable spell that music will at times cast over the minds of the most indifferent, now shed its glamour over her, and forced her to enter into the spirit of the song.

In a subdued tremulous voice she commenced the first notes of her reply. Her perfect knowledge of the language, and her keen perception of the awkwardness of the coincidence produced by the subject of the duet, had the effect of causing her to sing it with the most singularly appropriate style and expression; rather unfortunate under the circumstances. Her hesitation at first was just as it should be; and when, gathering courage, and inwardly resolving to dismiss from her imagination every idea but that she was expressing the sentiments of an ordinary love song, she ceased to think of Count Salvi or anything but what was written on the page before her; her tones became full and impassioned, her eyes sparkled, and her cheek flushed; and as the breach between the mythic lovers was gradually healed, and a triumphant reconciliation took place, her glorious voice rang out in a volume that amazed everyone present, and made them feel as if never until now had they done justice to her magnificent powers.

She was overwhelmed with compliments. A murmured sound of "Bellissima! bellissima!" fell faintly on her ear; but she sought not to trace from whence it came, and Count Salvi's attention seemed riveted on a piece of music that was lying on a table near them.

In silent ecstasy Marian had listened to singing such as she had never previously heard; and with bated breath she had leant eagerly forward that she might not lose one tone.

When it was over she gave a long sigh of mixed regret and relief; and turning suddenly towards Sir Charles Bellingham, she was on the point of appealing to him for sympathy in her pleasurable emotions, when the words were arrested on her lips by the look of angry annoyance visible on his countenance. His usually pleasant expression was completely gone; and in its place was a stern air of determination and a compression of the lips that alarmed as much as it astonished poor Marian, who for a moment spoke not a word, but gazed on him as if he had been a basilisk.

"Oh! Charles!" she exclaimed, "how you frighten me! What is it! What has vexed you?"

"Do I look vexed, Marian? Well, perhaps I am a little annoyed," and he bit his lip to restrain his rising irritation; "but one should not show such things in public."

"Never mind that, Charles; I daresay nobody saw it but me; but do tell me what it was that annoyed you? Was it — Augusta—singing that song?" she continued, a sudden light breaking in on her, for she remembered how he had talked of Count Salvi only a short time previously.

"Yes, Marian, it was that. I do not like it now; and I will not have it;" he replied with a momentary impetuosity.

"I am so sorry, Charles," said Marian gently—"so very sorry; and I am sure Augusta will be so too when she knows that you disapproved of it." Had the little girl been an acute observer she might have detected an expression of incredulity pass over her future brother-in-law's features; but she perceived nothing, and continued in a pleading voice—"but you will tell her of it, Charles? Of course she will stop it directly. She used to sing with him so much, that perhaps it never occurred to her to imagine you might not wish it now."

Sir Charles bent his eyes on her as he listened; and after she had ceased he looked at her curiously for a few moments before replying.

"I have heard tell of people who were too good for this world," he remarked at length; "but not many of them have crossed my path, Marian. If such characters do really exist, you are one of them, my dear little sister."

"There, now; you are quite yourself again, only you must not talk nonsense!" she replied, with her usual pretty blush, feeling excessively relieved to see his disturbed look pass away.

"It is not nonsense, Marian. I think you are an angel if ever there was one."

A sound as if of quick, repressed breathing, and Augusta stood before them, calm, but deadly pale, with an expression in her dark, unfathomable eyes not very good to see.

"Papa wishes you to sing something," she said, quietly addressing her sister. "You had better do so now."

"Very well," replied Marian, with a new and undefinable dread, for Augusta's manner and appearance troubled her. She rose and followed her sister to the piano, trembling very much at the prospect of singing before so many strangers. Her father met her with an encouraging smile, and taking her by the hand, he introduced her to Count Salvi, who bowed low and formally as they were named to each other.

"You must not expect anything very grand from this little English linnet," said Sir John, kindly: "but it has a sweet little pipe, too, and I am very fond of listening to it. Sing the 'Soldier's Tear,' my love; it is an especial favourite of mine."

Marian obeyed, and commenced, falteringly at first, gaining more courage as she proceeded; till at last her sweet, bird-like tones rang out soft and clear. Many flattering speeches greeted her when she finished.

"I would not give a song like that for all the Italian music that ever was written," exclaimed Sir Charles Bellingham frankly; "I never feel my nationality more strongly than in the matter of music. I back an English ballad against the world."

He had approached the group gathered round the musicians, and addressed his observation more especially to Mr. Talbot.

"I cordially agree with you," replied the old gentleman; "but that is rather a treasonable speech for you to make before you have converted Augusta to your way of thinking."

Miss de Burgh, who was seated on an ottoman beside them, smiled superciliously, but vouchsafed no glance in their direction.

"I really beg your pardon, Augusta," said Sir Charles heartily—"I am afraid that was rather a rude speech of mine, considering your *penchant* for Italian music. But after all, 'honesty is the best policy;' I do like English ballads best, and perhaps some day you will do so too."

"I am quite sure I shall not," replied Augusta, with freezing indifference. "I hope my taste may never deteriorate quite to that point."

She spoke low but distinctly, and Sir Charles heard her perfectly, as she meant he should do.

For a moment he looked astonished, then he perceived that her rudeness was intentional, and he walked away lest his irritation might prompt him to reply in a manner which he might afterwards regret.

"I wonder if your daughter and Count Salvi could be prevailed on to sing again?" remarked the ambassadress to Sir John de Burgh, beside whom she was sitting. "One has not often the privilege of hearing anything so perfectly lovely as their united voices."

To slip unperceived from her chair, to glide past the group round the piano, till she had reached the ottoman on which her sister was seated, was with Marian hardly the work of a moment.

Augusta was conversing with the Comte de Mérincourt when her sister hastily took a place by her side; but he, seeing by the eager expression in Marian's countenance that she had something important to communicate, at once bowed with ceremonious politeness, and retired.

"How can you act so very strangely, Marian?" said Augusta, coldly; "did you not observe that I was speaking to Monsieur de Mérincourt?"

"Oh! yes, I did," replied Marian, almost breathless with anxiety; "but Augusta, I wanted so much to tell you something, I could not wait another moment."

"Indeed! and pray what is this very interesting piece of information?" and Miss de Burgh spoke even more icily than before.

"Don't sing another duet with Count Salvi, Augusta; pray, don't?" and Marian whispered this with urgent entreaty, for she saw her father preparing to cross the room.

"Indeed! and why not, may I ask?" said

Augusta haughtily. "Oh! I understand; it is not agreeable to Sir Charles Bellingham. Is that the reason—and did he tell you so?"

She suddenly turned round and faced her sister with a look before which poor Marian trembled and shivered.

"I—I know he does not like it, Augusta," she replied timidly; "he—he was—annoyed about it last time. Oh! Augusta, please don't sing with him again; do make some excuse—say you are tired."

"I am not tired, Marian; and I will act as I choose, and sing with whom I please; and you can tell him so," said Augusta resolutely. "You and he seem to understand each other most thoroughly; pray, did he desire you to say this to me? because, if he did——"

"He did not—indeed he did not," whispered Marian, in an agony, for she saw her father approaching them—"but Augusta! indeed he does not like it; I know he does not—I am certain it will vex him greatly——." She was compelled to stop, for Sir John was standing beside the ottoman.

"Augusta," he said, "if you are not too

much exhausted by your last performance, there is a request for another duet."

Marian's imploring glance was utterly unheeded. Miss de Burgh rose gracefully from her seat, and walking straight to the piano, was immediately joined there by the Count. Marian remained behind in silent dismay and sorrow. So distressed was she by what had occurred that she sat plunged in a dark and dreamy reverie, so profound that she would scarcely have known that the duet was finished had not the clapping of hands at its close roused her to momentary observation; and then she remembered that the deed was done, and felt that she would have given anything in the world, had only she been able to have prevented it.

Still absorbed in her uncomfortable reflections, she presently became aware that Sir Charles Bellingham had seated himself beside her, though for several minutes he maintained a profound silence.

" Marian," he said, at length, in a low but firm voice, " I am going home now; but before leaving I wish to ask you just one question, and all the reply I require to it is 'yes' or 'no.' Will you answer me truly?"

"Yes, Charles, I will;" and she raised her eyes to his face as if in gentle deprecation of his impending inquiry.

"I saw you cross over to where your sister was sitting," he continued, "and there you spoke to her very earnestly. Now, Marian, tell me, truly, were you then informing Augusta that you knew I disliked her singing duets with Count Salvi? 'Yes' or 'no,' Marian; it is all I ask."

Poor Marian's tell-tale air would have been sufficient reply without the faint "yes" that came from between her trembling lips.

"Oh! yes, Charles, I was telling her," she continued, looking as though she, and not Augusta, were the guilty one; "but papa interrupted us before I had said more than a few words; and then it would have been very difficult indeed for her to refuse him, you know. She could hardly help herself; could she, Charles?"

"Marian," he replied, with a half-pitying smile, "you are prevaricating, you wicked little sinner, and you know it. It has too tender a little heart to betray its own sister, and I will not force it to do so; but I was watching the scene, and I am able to form my own conclusions on the subject. I shall speak to Augusta myself; she shall not offend again through ignorance of my feelings or wishes on the matter. So, good-night, dear, I shall slip away without further ceremony. You can make my excuses if they are needed." So saying, he rose, and in another minute he had quitted the room.

The party broke up soon afterwards; and, beyond some trifling remarks from Sir John, no one said anything respecting the absence of Sir Charles Bellingham.

Augusta did not allude to him in the faintest manner, though Marian anxiously hoped she might do so, and give her an opportunity of speaking on that and one or two other subjects that were weighing heavily on her mind.

But at length she saw very plainly that her sister was resolutely avoiding all possibility of being alone with her, even for a moment; and, very sadly, poor Marian owned this to herself, and felt that for the present, at least, she was utterly powerless—she could do nothing to clear up the misunderstanding that had arisen between Augusta and herself.

Her sister's parting salutation that night was as frigid as words could make it; and many a sad tear that, and the other incidents of the evening, cost poor Marian, when, alone in her room, she sat dejectedly turning the subject over in her mind, and pondering over the strange mystery that her own only sister did not, and she feared now, never would, love her.

But mournful as was the nature of her meditations, they were as nothing in comparison to the avalanche of bitterness and fury that seemed, as it were, to have crushed to the very earth the proud soul of Augusta, as she paced her chamber with hasty steps, her eyes gleaming with repressed passion, her small hands clenched as though she could have struck from her path any object, whatever it might be, that but for an instant dared to oppose her progress.

Had Marian—had Sir Charles Bellingham only seen her then, they would have
shrunk from her, appalled; so utterly
changed was she from the stately woman,
so calmly defiant, who had moved through
the brilliant *salon* scarcely an hour before.
More like a beautiful fury, or one possessed
by an evil spirit, she looked now, as, with
her dark hair hanging all dishevelled, her
neck and arms bare—for the fever raging in
her veins made her discard every covering—
her hands now thrown wildly in the air, now
pressed convulsively upon her throbbing
temples, she paced unceasingly up and down.

At length the frenzy of her mad passion
utterly exhausted her; and trembling, and
half-faint with sheer fatigue, she sank into
an arm-chair against which she had rested
for a moment, and remained for a long time
silent and motionless.

The clock on her chimney-piece striking
the hour warned her at length how much
of the night had passed. Rousing herself
from her reverie, she undressed hurriedly,
and threw herself wearily on her bed, to
snatch a disturbed and fitful slumber.

CHAPTER XI.

Augusta had a headache on the following morning, and did not make her appearance at breakfast; and before she had quitted her room there arrived for her a note from Sir Charles Bellingham. Marian would have taken it upstairs herself, and visited her sister in her own apartment; but Augusta's maid informed her that her mistress had particularly desired she might not be disturbed, so she had to resign the note to Pauline.

From some observations of her father's she concluded that Sir Charles had a long private interview with Augusta in the course of the forenoon; but he did not join their party at luncheon, and neither he nor Miss de Burgh went out riding during the day. Sir John and Marian rode as usual; and on returning to the house found Augusta in the *salon*, a light shawl marking her character of invalid, which was indeed not belied by her pallid countenance and heavy eyes.

"Dear Augusta, how ill you look!" said Marian compassionately; "is there nothing that I can do for you? I would not have gone out, had I known you were so poorly."

"I did not sleep very well last night," replied Augusta, with a languid smile; "that I daresay assisted to knock me up, but I shall soon be myself again."

"I am afraid we induced you to sing too much last night," observed her father kindly. "You were in such excellent voice, that perhaps we were rather unmerciful."

Augusta made no reply, but Marian saw a flush come into her cheek for a moment, and then fade away again, leaving it paler than before.

Presently she addressed herself to Marian— "I was sorry when I heard that Pauline had denied you admittance this morning; but I—I fancied that I might perhaps sleep, and had given orders not to be disturbed."

"It was of no consequence whatever," replied Marian; "I merely wished to inquire for you, and should have been greatly vexed had I roused you."

Augusta made no allusion to the note from Sir Charles Bellingham, nor did Marian; indeed she felt quite a nervous dread of approaching that subject. Her sister's manner puzzled her; it was gentle, almost kind, an amazing contrast to the angry pride and cutting disdain of the previous night; and Marian could not imagine by what agency so marvellous a change had been accomplished. They dined alone, but later in the evening Sir Charles joined their circle, his ostensible excuse being to inquire for Augusta. She was reclining on a sofa a little apart; and Sir Charles seated himself beside her, and talked to her in a low voice for some time.

In a high white dress, with a scarlet cashmere just resting on her rounded shoulders, Augusta looked very graceful and interesting.

Before long her late air of languor had entirely disappeared, and a bright glow of pleasure had taken its place; she was thoroughly metamorphosed by the potent wand of the mighty enchanter.

Marian witnessed the change with delight, and looked scarcely less beaming and happy than her sister. Bending over a portfolio of engravings, she felt more comfortable than she had done for many a day, when she was suddenly aroused from an agreeable reverie by hearing Augusta calling to her softly—"Marian, come here."

Rising at once, she went quickly towards the sofa, where Sir Charles Bellingham was already placing a chair for her.

"You must come and listen to my full, true, and particular confession, Marian," observed Augusta, with a bright smile; "I am here enacting the *rôle* of the Fair Penitent; and as you came in for a share of my misdeeds, as well as monsieur there, I appoint you both father confessors; premising that

my absolution is to be of the most handsome
description, no penances of any kind being
attached to it."

She spoke apparently with light and careless gaiety, but there was a restless glitter
in her eye that struck Marian painfully, she
scarcely knew why; and she could not help
fancying that the smile that wreathed Augusta's lip was more studied than if it had
been the artless expression of a tranquil
mind, pleased with itself and with everything around it.

"To-night I am the good child of the
story books," continued Augusta, with a
saucy laugh; "last night I was that unlucky
young person whose nurses assure her she
will be carried off by black men and de-
voured by ogres; now I am powerfully impressed with the extreme wickedness of my
behaviour, and I am never going to do so
no more! Italian duets are strictly pro-
hibited; English ballads are to receive
careful cultivation (you must give me some
lessons, Marian), and above all we are never
to be cross any more, and if in a moment

of aberration we find we are just going to say something naughty, the multiplication table is to be repeated backwards and forwards till the wicked impulse is entirely quenched. Now, Charles, have not I repeated my lesson quite correctly, and not forgotten a single word of it ?"

As she sat there with a half mocking light in her splendid eyes, and the smile of a siren on her chiselled lip, she looked so brilliantly beautiful that nothing in the guise of a man could for an instant have gainsaid her.

Sir Charles shook his head with an expression partly of amusement, partly of vexation; it was not the confession he had expected or hoped for; but, such as it was, it was an intimation of regret for what had taken place, and well—well, there was no help for it; it must e'en be allowed to pass.

Marian felt a little puzzled and pained by the scene before her; and she remained silent, not knowing what reply she was expected to make.

" Well, Marian," said Augusta, turning

towards her, with what even Marian could see was affected playfulness; "have you nothing to say to me? I hope I am quite discharged from your black books now?"

Every feature beamed, and the tone of her voice was as clear and ringing as usual; but though she smiled gaily, and her brow looked smooth and untroubled, there was an expression in her eyes, far down in their lustrous depths, that struck Marian strangely even then, and haunted her still more painfully afterwards.

"Oh! Augusta!" she said, the ready tear starting to her eye as she spoke, "you never were in my black books: I hope you did not really believe such a thing."

"Then if I were not, I ought to have been," replied Augusta, still in the same style of assumed *badinage*. "I know I spoke and acted like a perfect savage last night. I am quite shocked at the mere remembrance of it."

"I know you did not really mean what you said," remarked Marian earnestly: "perhaps—perhaps—it was my fault"—and then she turned very red, and hesitated:

for willing as she was to take to herself any possible or imaginable blame, the nature of her transgression did not distinctly present itself to her.

"There, now," said Augusta, with a slight laugh, "we will dismiss the subject, and have no further discussion about it. I think, Charles, if you were to fetch the chessboard over here, I might be tempted to try if I cannot beat you to-night. I feel rather in the mood for it."

Sir Charles obeyed her at once; and Marian only waited till all was comfortably arranged, and the game commenced; and then she returned to her portfolio, or, more truly, to her meditations, which were not interrupted until the dispersion of their circle for the night.

In the general confusion caused by moving about the room, and bidding adieu, Sir Charles contrived to have a few moments of private conversation with Marian.

"It is all right now," he said, cheerfully; "we had it out this morning after breakfast. I spoke very plainly, for I thought it was best to have no half measures. She behaved beautifully, and agreed to everything I wished."

"I am so glad, so very glad," replied Marian. "I was certain, if you only expressed your feeling to her yourself, she would yield at once."

"Well, you were quite right, little Marian," he observed, smiling; "and when we were on the subject, I put in a word for you. I thought she was inclined to be a trifle hard on you last night; your face is a sad little tell-tale; and she allowed she had been so, and that she had since regretted it very much."

" Oh! it was nothing worth mentioning," said Marian, lightly; " but I am so glad you and she have arranged matters nicely; and I am sure Augusta will be quite willing to avoid what you dislike, now that she knows it."

" What! more conspiracies!" exclaimed Miss de Burgh, in a gay tone, as she came across the room and joined them; " I shall quite expect to have to unravel some very formidable plot, if you two lay your heads together so frequently. Come, Charles, I shall be in Lady Agnes's blackest books if you linger here any longer. I must really warn you off the premises."

"Indeed, I fear I have shown myself very inconsiderate by remaining so long already," replied Sir Charles; "I ought to have remembered your headache, and advised early retirement. My only excuse is that you look so little of an invalid that the fact of your being one quite escaped my memory."

On retiring to their rooms the sisters chanced to ascend the staircase together. "Goodnight, Marian," said Augusta, stopping for a moment at the door of her own apartment.

The tone was languid and indifferent enough; but Marian, acting on the impulse of her enthusiastic nature, threw her arms fondly round her sister's neck, saying, "Goodnight, dear Augusta: I am so happy that you have made it all up again, and I hope you do not mind what I said to you last night: I am so very sorry if it vexed you."

"Well, Marian," replied Augusta, as she

coldly disengaged herself from her sister's clasp, "since you have mentioned the subject, I may as well tell you that I exceedingly dislike any interference with what only concerns myself; and for the future I shall be obliged if you will cease to interest yourself quite so keenly as you seem to do, in Sir Charles Bellingham's affairs and mine. We are quite competent to manage them ourselves: and I at least do not feel grateful to any one for interposition, however well meant it may be."

Speech and manner were both so utterly heartless and ungracious, that poor Marian fell back from her sister as if she had been stung; and it was with the greatest difficulty that she prevented herself giving way to a passionate burst of weeping, so grievous was the shock she had received.

But even the trodden worm will turn on the heel that crushes it; and Marian's gentle nature was at last roused to something like indignation at the chilling indifference to her love manifested by Augusta.

Resolutely forcing back her tears, and struggling to subdue the choking inclination she felt in her throat, she strove to answer calmly, while her poor little heart was beating almost to suffocation. "I beg your pardon, Augusta. I am very sorry that I have annoyed you, but I had no intention of doing so; and—and—I will be very careful for the future."

Tears, that would not be checked, were fast filling the bright eyes now; and by the end of her sentence her voice was becoming husky and broken.

"I did not mean to hurt your feelings, Marian," said Augusta, composedly. "I know your intentions were good; but now that you have learnt my dislike to all interference, I am sure you will endeavour to abstain from it. Now, good night, dear; go to sleep, and forget this little unpleasantness."

"More easily said than done," thought Marian to herself, as she felt her sister's lips pressed for a moment against her burning check; after which, Augusta turned coldly away, and entered her room, and Marian, with a bursting sob, sought her own chamber.

CHAPTER XII.

A MORNING VISIT, AND WHAT CAME OF IT.

A MORNING or two after this, the sisters set out on foot shortly after breakfast, in company with Mrs. Talbot, to make a few purchases in the Corso. The bright sunshine tempted them to prolong their walk, and Mrs. Talbot expressing a desire to call on Lady Agnes Bellingham, they turned their steps in the direction of her apartments. They were admitted, after a moment of hesitation on the part of the servant, which was partly accounted for when they reached the room in which the old lady was seated. The blinds were tightly drawn down, so as to exclude all but the faintest ray of light; and Lady Agnes was sitting with her back to the window, and a silk shade so fixed over her eyes as still further to diminish all risk of annoyance from a stray sunbeam. She rose to receive them, holding out both hands in token of kindly welcome.

"My dear Lady Agnes! what is the matter?" exclaimed Augusta, as she groped her way across the darkened room.

"Don't you know? Then you have not seen Charles; he left a short time ago, and said he should call and tell you of my misfortune," replied Lady Agnes, shaking hands with her visitors. "A little dust or something of the sort got into my eye yesterday afternoon, and the doctor has ordered me in consequence to take up my abode among the shades for a day or two."

"I am very sorry for it," observed Mrs. Talbot, compassionately; "and I trust it may last no longer than a day or two. I am glad we happened to call here this morning, as when Sir Charles is absent you must find the time hang rather heavy on your hands."

"Fortunately, I am very fond of knitting," replied Lady Agnes, exhibiting the dim outline of a stocking; "and that requires no particular exertion of the eyesight. But visitors are a pleasant variety, and an excuse for perfect idleness."

For more than an hour they remained with Lady Agnes, chatting over any little incidents occurring in their social circle, and discussing the approaching ceremonies of the Holy Week. Though greatly interested in the coming festival, Marian joined but seldom in the conversation; one idea was at the present moment predominant in her mind; a scheme had rapidly suggested itself to her, which she only hesitated to put into execution till she saw whether Augusta had not, as a matter of propriety and inclination, immediately decided on the same course.

At last, Mrs. Talbot rose to depart; and Miss de Burgh, after affectionately saluting her future mother-in-law, remarked, in a half hesitating tone, " It seems selfish to deprive you of Charles this afternoon, Lady Agnes; he means to ride with us, I know, but perhaps you cannot spare him. Shall we send him back to you?"

"On no account, my dear Augusta," replied Lady Agnes decidedly; "I can spare him perfectly; and the poor boy would not know what on earth to do with himself sitting with me in this dungeon. I have my knitting and shall manage very well; and for once in a way I dare say I shall find my own reflections very good company. Besides, it is quite time I should begin gradually to accustom myself to solitude; as it will soon be my fate to have a good deal of it."

There was a shade of sadness in her voice that touched the tender heart of Marian, as she stood there half irresolute in the purpose she had formed; and she marvelled whether the same idea had not struck Augusta that had occurred to herself. But no; Miss de Burgh did not press the matter further: and after announcing to Mrs. Talbot that she was perfectly ready to accompany her, she prepared once more to feel her way in the direction of the door. Marian saw that she must hesitate no longer.

"Lady Agnes," she murmured faintly, for she felt almost as if she were trespassing on the especial domain of Augusta, " may I —would you mind my remaining with you this afternoon? I should like it so very much if you will only let me."

" Let you, my dear !" said Lady Agnes warmly, " it will be the greatest possible pleasure to me ; only I feel it would be very selfish in me to deprive you of your ride for the sole purpose of sitting in a dark room with a stupid old woman.   Thank you all the same for your kind offer; it was very good of you to make it."

She had taken the young girl's hand in hers, and while she was speaking she kept stroking and fondling it; for short as was the time she had known Marian, Lady Agnes had, like others, found that her heart warmed to her more strongly and naturally, than was the case with respect to that grand and beautiful young lady her son's chosen bride.

" But I should like so much to stay, Lady Agnes," persisted Marian; "indeed, I should not enjoy my ride at all when I thought of you sitting here all alone in the dark.   I am sure papa would prefer that I should remain here: don't you think he would, grandmamma?"

Thus appealed to, Mrs. Talbot replied, "I am quite certain he would, my dear; and I think Lady Agnes will consent to allow you to bear her company. You must summon up your best conversational powers for her entertainment. She can be a regular little chatter-box sometimes I assure you, Lady Agnes; though one might imagine she had left her tongue at home this morning."

"I don't doubt but we shall get on very well," said Lady Agnes, kindly; "and I shall no longer deny myself the gratification of keeping this willing little hostage, as she insists upon relinquishing her ride. But I fear, my dear, that your only compensation will be the consciousness of having performed a very charitable action. I shall take good care of you, and Charles shall escort you home himself, and restore you in perfect safety." She smiled and patted softly the little trembling hand still enclosed in her own; and once more Mrs. Talbot said adieu, and then addressed her elder granddaughter, saying, "Now Augusta, my dear, I think we had better be going."

"Very well, grandmamma," observed Miss de Burgh, quietly, "I am quite ready."

It was, perhaps, well for them all that the obscurity of the room prevented them seeing distinctly the countenance of Augusta.

When first the nature of her sister's proposal had dawned upon her, a cloud of stormy indignation had settled on her brow, which, as the little discussion continued, gave place to a deep-seated expression of bitter scorn and aversion.

She saw clearly that the suggestion which had just emanated from Marian, ought unhesitatingly to have proceeded from herself; but she had allowed the golden opportunity to slip, which now that it had escaped her grasp, she felt that she would willingly concede a great deal to have once more placed within her reach; but it was too late now, and she could only show her displeasure with her sister by a chilling farewell, when she and her grandmother finally took their departure for home.

"There! I have vexed Augusta again," sadly reflected poor Marian, as she listened to their retreating footsteps: "but why should she be angry with me now?" And the deep sigh that escaped her at this thought attracted the attention of Lady Agnes.

"Not regretting your seclusion already, my dear?" she said, in a playful tone, kindly embracing the young girl as she spoke. "That tremendous sigh rather alarms me for your powers of endurance."

"Oh! no, Lady Agnes, I am not at all afraid of being tired; I was only—only—thinking of something."

"And of something not very lively apparently, to judge from the result," said the old lady cheerfully. "I don't like to hear little girls like you, who should be as gay and merry as birds, sighing in a way that only old women such as I am have any right to dream of doing—if, indeed, old women are at all entitled to sigh any more than young ones. No one should ever resign themselves hopelessly to the depressing influence of sorrow. Believe me, my dear, that our cares are generally sent to us as lessons; and the trouble that is bravely met and borne has its weight half lightened by such submissive fortitude."

"That may be true of many sorrows, Lady Agnes, but surely not of all?"

"Of every one, I think I may say, my dear, if only we take pains to regard the matter in the proper light. If among our roses we now and then find some thorns, we must strive to bear them with courage, and not give way to grief and despondency. You must not take my little sermon amiss;" and Lady Agnes, who had seated herself on a sofa by her young visitor, put her arm kindly round her, and kissed her with much affection.

"Oh! no, dear Lady Agnes. I should never think of such a thing," replied Marian eagerly, at the same time pressing the old. lady's hand warmly within her own. "I think it is very good of you to speak to me as you are now doing; for I have no one to give me advice, or that I can speak to as I feel I may to you. I have no one to give me advice," she repeated, in a melancholy tone; "for though no person could possibly be fonder of me or more devoted to me than dear grandmamma, I think she considers me a child still, and treats me more as a little girl than a grown-up one."

"You are not very old yet, my dear," replied Lady Agnes, kindly—"but you are just at that period of life when a young girl most misses the tender care of a mother. It is a very loving and beautiful tie that unites a mother and a daughter. I had a little girl once; she was not unlike you, Marian. Your blue eyes and golden hair have often brought back to my memory the days now so long ago when my sunny little Blanche used to play beside me—a merry, happy little creature she was. I do not speak unadvisedly when I tell you that very heavy afflictions may leave only gentle traces behind. I have known much sorrow, Marian, and yet I am neither desponding nor unhappy."

"Oh! Lady Agnes, if I could only feel about things as you do," exclaimed Marian

eagerly; " if I could only talk to you sometimes, I am sure I should be better and
happier."

" Then, my dear, I hope you will do so
whenever you feel inclined; it cannot be a
greater pleasure to you than it will be to
me.   You will find me at all times willing
to bestow advice upon you to the best of my
power—advice such as your own dear mother
would have given to her daughters had she
been spared to watch over them."

" I shall most gladly avail myself of your
kind offer," replied Marian, gratefully; " but
I fear you will find me very troublesome."

" I am not afraid of that, my dear: the
oftener you come to me the better pleased
I shall be.   And now, don't you think you
would be more comfortable were you to
remove your bonnet and shawl?   Let me
ring and desire my maid to take them away,
and then we shall have a much more snug
and sociable appearance. Charles dines from
home to day, otherwise I should have proposed your remaining to share our family
dinner, if you are not otherwise engaged."

"But that makes it all the more necessary that I should stay with you," replied Marian. "I have no engagement, so I hope you will invite me to dinner with you: if you don't I shall invite myself."

"My dear, I cannot think of permitting you to sacrifice your entire day to me in this manner."

"It is a sacrifice, however, that I am quite determined to make," said Marian, laughing; "and you don't know how positive I can be sometimes, Lady Agnes. The only thing is, I must tell them not to expect me at home until the evening."

"I shall send a message to say so," replied Lady Agnes; "and now here is Carson for your bonnet."

The little change was soon effected; Marian declined all offers of a mirror, and smoothing down her rippling braids with her hands, she drew forward a stool beside the chair of Lady Agnes, and announced her intention of having a regular afternoon of gossip.

And very pleasantly the hours slipped

away; no feeling of weariness was experienced either by the old lady or the young one. From one subject they wandered to another; grave topics gave place to gay ones, gossip was succeeded by discussions of a more serious nature; and the close of the afternoon found Lady Agnes and her young companion on a very different footing of regard and intimacy from anything that had previously existed between them; and when Sir Charles returned home he found his mother and her young visitor still in friendly confabulation; he could just distinguish the dark figures by the faintly flickering sparkle of the small wood fire.

"This is very kind of you, Marian," he exclaimed, coming towards them, and greeting her warmly; "my mother and I are both greatly indebted to you."

"Pray don't say so," replied Marian, "I have spent the most delightful afternoon possible."

"Then you have yourself caused it to be so, my dear," remarked Lady Agnes; "virtue has been its own reward in your case. But I am glad you have not found it very dull; you have made the time pass most pleasantly to me."

"I can well believe it," said Sir Charles, glancing for a moment at the graceful figure on the stool, "and I am sure Marian has been very happy in the performance of her good deed; but it strikes me that it was more the place of Augusta to stay with my mother than you, Marian, and I told her so during our ride."

"Oh, Charles, did you?" exclaimed Marian, in an uneasy tone; and then fearing she had said too much, she suddenly stopped, and remained silent.

"Indeed I did," replied Sir Charles, rather hotly. "Augusta is not at all so ready to consider others as she might be; and under the circumstances I should have felt gratified had she volunteered to bear my mother company this afternoon. It would only have been a proper mark of attention on her part."

"Hush, Charles," said Lady Agnes, gently, for Marian was too pained and uncomfortable to make the slightest remark; "you forget in your sympathy with my misfortune that Augusta may probably have hesitated to deprive you of her company in your ride. Your claim on her attention is superior to any that I may have; indeed, I would not have consented to her remaining with me; and I positively refused to accede to her wish that you should stay at home. The reward of my unselfishness has been a very charming visit from Marian; and I assure you I have been much too well off in securing her company to regret the absence of any one else —yourself into the bargain, Master Charles."

This rather lengthy harangue was partly intended to allow of Sir Charles cooling down a little; as on Marian's account she dreaded a continuance of the discussion, which she felt must be distressing her greatly.

"Well, well, mother, I shall say no more about it, except again to express my cordial thanks to Marian;" observed Sir Charles, in some degree divining her intentions. "And how is the *casus belli*, which I have un- pardonably neglected all this time—much better, I hope?"

"I have no pain now," replied Lady Agnes; "it has gradually disappeared beneath the spell of our pleasant little gossip."

"You must both be pretty nearly cat's-eyed I should fancy," said her son, laughing. "If I attempted to cross the room without feeling my way, I should inevitably break my neck. When am I to have the honour of escorting you home, Marian? I received very strict injunctions on the subject from Mrs. Talbot, with a list of special directions as to wrapping you up properly, which I mean to attend to in person."

"But I am going to dine here, and stay all the evening," replied Marian; "Lady Agnes and I arranged that after grandmamma left us."

"I sent a message to Sir John de Burgh's to that effect," said Lady Agnes. "When Marian heard that you were going out to dinner, she insisted on spending the rest of the day with me. But I hope, Charles, that you will return here in good time to escort her home; I promised Mrs. Talbot that you should do so."

"I shall most certainly escort her home, mother; make your mind quite easy on that score. Let me see, now—what o'clock is it?" He stooped towards the flickering firelight, and with some difficulty deciphered the tiny figures on the dial of his watch. "Half-past five; at what hour do you dine, mother?"

"As you were from home, I ordered dinner at six," said Lady Agnes; "and as you do not dine till half-past seven, I shall be very glad if you will take charge of Marian, and I shall act up to my vocation of owl, and have a tray brought to me here. You will have ample time to dress afterwards; and my mind will be easy as to this good little Samaritan not being starved, which I think not an improbable result if no one looked after her but herself."

"I shall do so with pleasure," replied Sir Charles, a little absently. "Ah, dinner at six you said. Just excuse me for a few minutes, I shall not be away long."

He immediately quitted the room; but his absence was of longer duration than he had mentioned, for Luigi had already announced that dinner was in readiness before Sir Charles, with an apology for detaining them, hurriedly rejoined his mother and her young visitor. As he came forward to offer his arm to Marian, she observed that he was in evening costume.

"Dressed already," she remarked; "how very quick you have been."

"Rapid indeed," said Lady Agnes, laughing; "you don't in general exert yourself so marvellously. But I am very glad of it, for now you can stay with us till the last moment. Better go now, or the soup will be cold, and Luigi in despair."

"We shall not be long," said Marian, as she rose to accompany Sir Charles into the next room.

"Now, Charles, take very good care of her." The young couple laughed at her injunctions, and merrily fumbled their way between chairs and tables into the adjacent dining-room.

"Allow me to induct you into my mother's seat," said Sir Charles, as he led his fair

guest to the place at the top of the table.
"The effect is really admirable," he continued, as he assumed his position opposite
her; "it quite savours of a conjugal *tête-à-
tête.* I wonder what Luigi thinks of it.
Lady Bellingham," he added gaily, "may I
have the pleasure of sending you some soup?"

"I will have some, please," replied Marian,
blushing and giving him a glance of appealing warning, while she pointed for a
moment to Luigi, just then otherwise
occupied.

"Pooh: he doesn't understand English,"
remarked Sir Charles, carelessly; "he only
speaks Italian and French."

The dinner was a very merry one: the
young couple were perfectly lively and
unembarrassed, and more than once Marian
rallied Sir Charles on his politeness in considering it necessary that his companionship
should extend to eating and drinking, as
well as to conversation.

"What shall you do at your dinner party?"
she asked, laughingly; "you can't possibly have the slightest vestige of appetite."

"Well, probably not much," he replied, with rather a peculiar smile : "and Colonel Vivian has a first-rate cook. I shall not be very severe on the entrées to-day."

"What a pity you were engaged to him," said Marian : "it would be so nice if you had not to go away."

"Should you really be glad if I could have remained at home?" enquired Sir Charles rather eagerly, pausing for a moment, and looking her full in the face.

"Of course I should," replied Marian, frankly ; "why should you doubt it?"

"Then you will not feel so shocked at my taking a second supply of this *vol-au-vent*, when I inform you that I despatched my apologies to Colonel Vivian some time ago."

"Oh! Charles, did you?" and Marian smiled with an air of great satisfaction. "Lady Agnes will be so pleased : she will think it so kind of you."

"I did not do it entirely on my mother's account, sorella mia. I must not let you credit me with goodness equal to your own.

But my mother has caged a little bird this evening, whose sweet notes have a marvellous attraction for me; though, of course," he added, with affected gravity, " as a dutiful son, I am naturally much overcome by my fond parent's calamitous deprivation, and I feel impelled to offer her the inexpressible consolation of my society."

"Nonsense !" said Marian, with a smile; at the same time she blushed and looked considerably perplexed. " I hope you have not really stayed at home on my account, Charles?" she continued, with a deepening colour, and an air of anxiety; " I shall be much vexed if this is the case."

" Why should you be vexed, Marian?" he replied, warmly; " surely you do not imagine that I in the least regret missing the party —a bachelor dinner to begin with—but had it been the most splendid entertainment in Rome, I would have relinquished it freely to have the pleasure of spending my evening with you. You little know what your companionship is to me; this sweet sisterly intercourse that has begun to lend a new charm to my life. Marian! Marian! I sometimes think it had been better for my peace of mind had I seen you sooner, or never seen you at all!"

Dinner was over, and Luigi had quitted the room, when Sir Charles spoke those impetuous words.

He rose from his chair, and took a few hasty turns up and down; while Marian remained with her eyes fixed on her plate, cold and hot by turns, totally unable to utter a syllable, and feeling most keenly the discomfort and awkwardness of her position.

And yet something must be done, something must be said; else how could she again raise her eyes to those of Sir Charles, how manage to conduct herself for the rest of the evening in such a manner as not to excite surprise or suspicion on the part of Lady Agnes, a catastrophe which filled Marian's mind with a sensation of perfect horror.

She felt as if rising from her seat, or even looking up for a moment, were thoroughly beyond her power; and the awful pause seemed to her of endless length, though, in reality, it had lasted but for a few minutes.

Presently, Sir Charles approached her chair, and said in a voice completely altered, humble and sorrowful, "Forgive me, Marian; I ought not to have spoken as I did just now. A sudden impulse came over me for a moment, and I forgot myself; but I regret it most deeply now. Say that you forgive me."

"I do, indeed, Charles," murmured the young girl, scarcely venturing to look up: "but please never speak to me so again. You will make me very miserable if you do."

"I never shall," replied Sir Charles, eagerly; "I grieve to think that I should have distressed you now. But it burst from me almost before I knew it; and I regretted it the instant that the words had crossed my lips. I shall never offend you so again, Marian."

"I am not offended, Charles," said Marian, gently; "but you must never allow yourself to draw comparisons between my sister and myself; it is doing a great injustice to us both.

You chose Augusta for your wife," here her listener winced; "and you must try never to think of her unkindly; it is not right that you should do so."

"Ah! Marian, if you only knew all," murmured Sir Charles in a tone hoarse with emotion: then the innate feeling of a gentleman restrained him, and he felt that he could not betray the woman who loved him.

Indeed at this moment he scarcely knew what he was saying or doing. When Marian had a little recovered from the painful awkwardness of her position, she was the more self-possessed of the two; and, as such, she saw that she must take the initiative in ending a scene that had already lasted far too long.

"We must return to Lady Agnes now," she observed, with an assumption of tranquillity which she was very far from feeling: "she will be wondering what has become of us. And oh! Charles, if you love me, as I think you do, never revert to this subject; never say anything that is disloyal to Augusta, for you to speak, or for me to hear.

On this condition alone will I continue to you the sisterly friendship which I have not doubted till this evening. Augusta may be erring at times; but she is my sister, and I will not be untrue to her."

"I fear she is no true sister to you, Marian, though you behave like an angel to her always; and to see this tries my feelings almost more than anything else," exclaimed Sir Charles, impulsively.

"Hush!" said Marian, raising a warning forefinger, and quitting her chair as she spoke; "I will listen to no more from you now, Charles: we must go to your mother."

The consciousness of right had invested the young girl with a dignity and fortitude that made her completely mistress of the situation. Never once had she allowed herself to think, that might be reserved for hereafter: at present she had only to act, and to act as should be wisest and best for them both.

In emergencies like this, women, even the youngest and most inexperienced, think and behave more judiciously than men. Their unerring tact, like a human instinct, impels them to the right course; often without their being able to explain it further than by urging the strong impulse that guided and directed their actions.

And so Marian de Burgh and her repentant companion returned to the *salon* where Lady Agnes Bellingham sat awaiting them.

"I am afraid we have remained a long time absent," said Marian, rather nervously; "the cook sent up such a variety of good things, and Luigi proffered them in such an appealing manner, that it was scarcely possible to resist him."

"I am glad you were taken care of," replied Lady Agnes, smiling; "and I hope that Charles also obeyed my injunctions and attended to you very faithfully."

"So faithfully, my dear mother, that eating another dinner, or even attempting to do so, would be a matter of sheer impossibility. Colonel Vivian will, therefore, not number me among his guests to-day; for though I will do much for my friends, a limit must be drawn somewhere, and it stops short at eating two dinners."

"You are surely joking, my dear Charles," said Lady Agnes, looking puzzled; "do you mean that you are not going to Colonel Vivian's?"

"Exactly so, mother; I propose to have the pleasure of passing the evening with you, if your ladyship has no objection to the arrangement."

"I shall be very much pleased to have your company, my dear boy, as you very well know; but do you not think Colonel Vivian may consider so tardy an apology rather impolite on your part?"

"Possibly he might," replied Sir Charles, smiling; "and as such a reflection would inevitably destroy the harmony of our evening, I shall relieve your mind by mentioning that the gallant officer received my note of excuse a considerable time ago."

Lady Agnes Bellingham was an old lady of a very acute and observant turn of mind, and one who was able to form very rapid conclusions from premises apparently trifling and unimportant.

Under her green silk shade her bright piercing eyes wore a reflective and puzzled expression, and a cloud of grave anxiety rested on the brow usually so serenely calm beneath the snowy badge of widowhood. Something in the voices and manner of the two young people struck her as being forced and unnatural; a very slight difference it might be, but even that was enough to make her wonder what could have caused it.

The time they had remained at dinner was much longer than their original intention; and now when they had returned, it seemed to Lady Agnes that their remarks proceeded from an apparent desire to make conversation and prevent a pause, which, for some reason or other, they mutually appeared to dread.

The fire had been replenished; fresh logs of pine wood were crackling merrily, and the room wore a very bright and cheerful aspect. Marian drew forward a low stool and seated herself before the fire in close proximity to Lady Agnes, making it appear as though she were chilly and wished to warm her fingers at the blaze; though this was more as an excuse for silence and to conceal the embarrassment which, in spite of herself, kept stealing over her, than from any real desire for warmth.   The old lady passed her hand caressingly over the soft silken tresses of her young guest, and wondered what had happened to check the gay flow of spirits that had so cheered her during the long afternoon; while Sir Charles leant back in a deep chair, and glanced furtively at Marian's golden hair gleaming in the firelight, envying his mother the privilege of stroking it, and longing, if only for a moment, to hold one stray lock in his fingers and raise it to his lips.

For as he sat there, joining only occasionally in the conversation maintained by his mother, and feebly responded to by Marian, it began gradually to dawn on the mind of the perplexed young man that he had committed a great mistake; he had bound himself to marry a woman whom he had never really loved; and now, having met one whom he felt that he could and did love, he had by his own act placed her for ever beyond his reach.

He gazed on the slight young form before him, so graceful and feminine, so entirely fulfilling his ideal of womanly loveliness; on the bending head with its glory of golden hair, on the face so fair and gentle, with its melting blue eyes and its winning expression of sweetness and innocence; and he knew as he looked, that in Marian de Burgh he had met with a woman who could make him perfectly happy, and yet that woman was as utterly beyond his reach, as though she had for ever remained a stranger to him in the quiet retirement of her distant English home.

Lady Agnes finding conversation very up-hill work, presently asked Marian to give them a little music; and as she willingly complied and rose from her position at the fire, Sir Charles proceeded at once to open the piano and adjust the stool for her.

To enable her to see better, the lamp was moved nearer the instrument, and its

outer edge of light just rested on the countenance of the young baronet as he seated
himself on a sofa, close to the stool occupied
by the fair musician. By an unlucky coincidence, just as Marian had sounded a few
preliminary chords, Lady Agnes begged her
to sing, " Josephine's Adieu to Napoleon."
It was a ballad she had often sung, and was
an especial favourite with Lady Agnes, so
there was nothing at all remarkable in her
asking for it now ; but poor Marian, remembering the tenor of the words, felt overpowered with a sensation of nervous confusion, and blushed so vividly and painfully,
that she felt thankful the shadow prevented
it from being observed. No possible excuse
for refusing presented itself to her mind; so
she played a short prelude, to give her a
few moments in which to gather courage,
and then she sang the sad and touching song.

Lady Agnes lay back in her chair and
listened; pleasantly the soft liquid notes
fell on her ear; to her such music was far
more attractive than the melodies of the
Italian and German schools, so exclusively

patronised by Augusta; and beautiful as she acknowledged her future daughter-in-law's voice to be, far sweeter, in her opinion, were the low and thrilling tones of her sister, when they were heard in those dear old ballads, that carried her back to happy days and scenes long ago.

Very similar thoughts were passing through the mind of her son as he too listened to the soft voice he loved so well; and as the song proceeded, and its tender sentiments sounded in his ear, he felt that if he could only believe such feelings might ever have a place in the heart of Marian de Burgh, he would scatter the past to the winds, and dare all to gain a love that would be to him a prize, such as it made him shrink and shiver to think was never by any possibility to be within his power.

And as he sat there, and thought all this, his eyes were riveted on Marian with a gaze of wistful intensity, a look that saw nothing in the room but the one figure at the piano, and heeded nought else that might be going on around him.

So that when something in his appearance, and the perfect stillness of his attitude, attracted the attention of Lady Agnes, she roused herself to observe him more narrowly; and one glance from those piercing eyes at the dejected countenance of the young man, one look at the yearning sadness reflected in his expression, and the secret of his altered manner, of his silence and abstraction, lay as completely unveiled to her as though he had himself laid bare his heart.

The shock to the devoted and affectionate mother was very great. For a few moments a mist seemed to float before her, making every object indistinct; her heart beat so painfully that she pressed her hand upon it, as if to still its too rapid pulsations, and she was compelled to lie back in the chair to allow herself to recover from a sensation of faintness that almost threatened to overpower her.

"I have so feared, so dreaded this," was her sorrowful reflection; "and it has come upon him! My boy—my own dear boy— God help you in this terrible trial!"

"Thank you, my dear," she murmured in a low voice, when the song came to a conclusion; and some almost inaudible words were also uttered by Sir Charles.

In this dark corner, where no uncomfortable scrutiny could put her out of countenance, Marian felt her lost courage gradually returning to her: she could not trace the sadness visible on the features of Lady Agnes, and in the direction of the young baronet she never once permitted her eyes to stray. So she continued to sit there, pouring forth one simple strain after another, as inclination or fancy suggested, till a considerable time had elapsed; and then suddenly rising, before her resolution should again fail her, she said, in a tone which she strove to render gay and cheerful—

"I must really stop now, for I think I have sung you both to sleep; but it was so pleasant singing in that kind of invisible manner."

Lady Agnes roused herself directly.

"I have not been asleep, my dear, though I have been so silent. Your sweet voice acted like a spell on me, and lulled me into a sort of dreamland. Singing often has that effect upon me, and yours more so than any I ever heard. There is such a home-like ring in your native wood-notes wild."

Then suddenly remembering that this remark was trenching on dangerous ground, she hastened to thank Marian, and then made way for her to return to her former position in front of the fire, whither she was followed by Sir Charles, who now strove with better success than before to assist in maintaining conversation.

Whilst thus engaged Luigi entered with coffee: and soon afterwards Lady Agnes's maid appeared to enquire whether "her lady-ship would not like a cup of tea."

"Oh! couldn't we have it in here, regu-larly on a table?" exclaimed Marian, glancing eagerly round the room to see which seemed most suitable for the purpose. "I have not seen such a thing since I came abroad; it would be like a sudden vision of dear Old England. I should so enjoy pouring it out: I always made tea at home—at Summerton."

Lady Agnes smiled at her childlike eagerness, and instantly desired Carson to give the necessary instructions. Before long Marian was seated at a small table covered with a white cloth, a glittering tea equipage before her, with the exception of the hissing urn, which Carson regretted was an article not included in the *mènage;* and which she had endeavoured to supply to the best of her ability by a massive silver jug of boiling water.

Pleased at the gratification of her little whim, Marian was again careless and happy as she had been in the earlier part of this eventful day; and she daintily rinsed out the cups and manipulated the lumps of sugar, laughing merrily as she did so, and declaring that she felt just as if she were sitting in their favourite oak parlour at Summerton.

The infection of her gaiety spread to the others, and a very cheerful party they soon formed : Marian insisting on attending to Lady Agnes herself, and placing a little table for her especially, just beyond the charmed circle of light formed by the lamp on the tea-table.

Marian's cheek glowed and her eyes sparkled; rarely had she looked more bewitching: Sir Charles could not withdraw his fascinated gaze from the charming face beside him, though he was careful not to permit Marian to perceive how intense was the admiration with which he regarded her.

But his mother saw it all; and her heart sunk within her as she read in his countenance the unmistakeable signs of a passion as profound as it was unfortunate.

But all wore the aspect of outward peace and enjoyment; Lady Agnes sat tranquilly smiling in her easy chair, and Marian's silvery laughter was ringing through the room as Sir Charles under her directions raised the huge silver tankard, not originally intended to serve as an adjunct to the tea-table, and proceeded to perform the important ceremony of " filling up the pot."

No sound or movement had given them the slightest warning of an approaching interruption, when the door of the apartment was suddenly thrown wide open, and Luigi's announcement of " Mademoiselle de Burgh," was almost instantaneously followed by the entrance of Augusta, in simple evening attire, over which she had carelessly thrown an opera cloak to protect her from the air during her short drive.

So utterly unexpected was her appearance, that for a few moments the group round the little tea-table remained as if paralysed, and not the faintest observation was made by any of the party.

Sir Charles, in unmistakeable confusion, continued steadily to pour water from the tankard; while Marian, with a burning blush that dyed cheeks, forehead, even her fair throat and shell-like ears all the same glowing hue, held open the lid with trembling fingers, till the running over of the teapot recalled her to a sense of the extreme absurdity of their position.

" I seem to have given you a surprise," remarked Augusta, as she coolly crossed the room and deposited her cloak on a sofa, while Sir Charles sprang forward to assist her; " I might almost have been a ghost, to judge from the effect I have produced."

She looked not unlike one as she stood facing them with eyes in which shone a terrible expression; the white dress which she wore not whiter than her haughty face, and both of them thrown more prominently into relief by the shadow that rested on that part of the room.

"Well, your entrance was undeniably after the manner of ghosts," replied Sir Charles, trying to speak lightly, but feeling that it was a complete failure, and that he was in truth looking horribly guilty.

"I did not expect to find you here," said his fiancée, regarding him steadily; "you told me you were engaged to dine with Colonel Vivian."

"I was," replied Sir Charles, "but I afterwards sent an apology. I thought my mother—" but at this point he stopped: not even to appease Augusta would he offer an excuse that was not genuine.

"Oh! I understand," observed Miss de Burgh with an almost imperceptible sneer in her tones; "you were seized with a sudden access of filial devotion very becoming on your part. Something of the same nature brought me here this evening, to surprise you all so agreeably. When the carriage was ordered to fetch Marian home, I felt impelled to come in person, and enquire for your eye, Lady Agnes. I hope it is now very much better?"

By a frightful exertion of her iron will she had now subdued her feelings sufficiently to speak with composure and even cheerfulness; but what the effort had cost her, her companions little guessed.

"It was very good of you to think of this, my dear Augusta," said Lady Agnes, kindly; in her heart feeling that she had perhaps been guilty of injustice to her future daughter-in-law, and now extremely anxious to make amends for the somewhat chilling reception the young lady had experienced. "A strong proof of my convalescence is the brightened aspect of affairs. As you may perceive, we have been introducing English fashions into Rome."

"Indeed you all look particularly comfortable; and I hope somebody intends to offer me a cup of tea?" observed Miss de Burgh, as she took the seat placed for her by Sir Charles.

"I am afraid it is very weak now," said Marian, who had in some measure recovered from her confusion; and she proceeded to examine the strength of the considerably diluted beverage.

"You acted exactly according to the *rôle* of heroines when taken aback," remarked Augusta, with a glance of piercing meaning at her sister, which once more dyed poor Marian's cheeks scarlet; "I see the tray is floating, from which I may draw a tolerable inference as to the excellence of your tea. None for me, thank you; and when you are ready to return home, I am at your service."

"I will go whenever you like," said Marian, timidly; "I am quite ready."

"Then, as the carriage is at the door, and your duties here appear to be completed, perhaps we had better not keep the horses waiting."

The pleasant, cheerful evening had been rudely broken up, and its bright, homelike visions dispelled; all felt that a return to their former condition was impossible, and neither Lady Agnes nor her son offered any opposition to the departure of the sisters.

Sir Charles carefully adjusted the opera cloak round the graceful shoulders of his future bride, and then turned to assist Carson in performing the same office for Marian, who nervously shrank from his touch.

A cold, passive kiss was exchanged between Lady Agnes and Augusta; and then Marian's warm lips were eagerly and lovingly pressed on the old lady's soft cheek, while she felt that Lady Agnes held her fondly to her heart ere she released her from her clasp.

Sir Charles gave his arm to Augusta, and escorted them down-stairs.

Marian hung behind, not to interrupt them in any private remarks that might not be intended for her ear; but her caution was totally unnecesary, Sir Charles merely observed in an audible manner that "it seemed a fine night;" while Augusta equally distinctly replied that "it was rather chilly;" and so, with perfectly calm and courteous adieux on both sides, they entered the carriage; and Sir Charles waved his hand to them as they slowly drove out of the court-yard.

CHAPTER XIII.

AUGUSTA waved her hand in return as the
carriage drove off; then drawing up the
window she leant back into her own corner,
and plainly announced by her manner that
she had no desire to enter into conversation
with her sister.   So the two returned home
in perfect silence.   On reaching the house
they proceeded at once to the *salon*, where
Sir John de Burgh and Mr. and Mrs. Talbot
were awaiting them, full of kind enquiries
for Lady Agnes Bellingham, and laughing
questions as to how she and Marian had
occupied themselves during the long hours of
darkness.   The pleasant home circle, and the
cheerful influence of kind voices and loving
looks, soon roused Marian from her tempo-
rary depression; and she laid aside her

bonnet and shawl, shook out her imprisoned curls, and began to give them what she called "a full, true, and particular account of everything."

"I found my tongue after you left, grand-mamma, and talked a very great deal, I assure you."

"I'll be bound you did," said Mr. Talbot, jocosely; "I will back you for a little chatter-box against all the young ladies in Rome."

"You wicked grandpapa, you know you are very fond of hearing me talk; and Lady Agnes paid me the compliment of telling me she had enjoyed my society very much indeed."

"You must have discussed a good many different subjects during such a prolonged sitting," remarked Sir John, looking at her kindly.

"Oh! yes, papa, quantities of things; it was so nice, sitting there talking in the dim firelight; and we never wearied in the very least. Lady Agnes asked me all about my life at home—at Summerton; and she told me about Bellingham Court—what a beautiful place it must be.   The park is ten miles round, papa, and quite full of deer; and there is a lake more than a mile long, covered with water-lilies, and a number of swans."

"I hope you are listening to this description of your future home, Augusta,"observed Mr. Talbot, addressing his elder grand-daughter; "Marian has the catalogue of its beauties by heart."   "She seems indeed to have been greatly interested," replied Augusta, in a tone of meaning of which poor Marian well understood the drift; after which remark Miss de Burgh resumed her occupation of writing at a small table, to which she had gone on entering the room, and Marian felt that any further description of Bellingham Court was out of the question, and led the conversation into other channels.

"I suppose Lady Agnes did not starve you?" asked Mr. Talbot, smiling; "it must have been rather hungry work speaking all day long."

"Oh! we had a capital dinner, all kinds of good things," replied Marian; "we took ours in the dining-room, but Lady Agnes was afraid of the light, so she had hers taken into the drawing-room.''

" Who were *we*?" inquired Sir John; "Sir Charles said he was going to dine at Colonel Vivian's."

"But he did not go after all," said Marian, feeling the · rebellious colour once more stealing over her face, and wishing most devoutly she had not made the unlucky slip.

"How was that?" observed her father: " he said nothing of sending an apology when he left us on our return home from riding."

All necessity for reply on the part of Marian was completely averted by a sudden catastrophe occurring at the table where her sister was writing. By a rapid motion of her arm Miss de Burgh had contrived to knock over one of the large Sèvres candle-sticks that stood beside her; and the crash of the shattered china startled the whole party, and every one advanced to the scene of the accident, by which interruption an entire cessation was put to the previous discussion.

" Dear me! It is later than I thought,"

said Mrs. Talbot, looking at her watch; " I think I shall wish you all good night." Suiting the action to the word she embraced Augusta, and then retired, accompanied by Marian, who made some inaudible remark about feeling rather sleepy, and departed in the wake of her grandmother.

When Marshall, who attended her, had accomplished her duties, and all was dark and silent in her chamber, Marian for the first time permitted her thoughts to stray back to the earlier part of the day, and take in review all that had occurred during the afternoon and evening. She thought over every little incident and circumstance in detail; and was relieved to find at the conclusion of her retrospect, that in no one way could she attach any shadow of blame to herself for anything that had unfortunately occurred.

Sir Charles's rash declaration had burst from him without her having the faintest idea beforehand that such a perplexing statement was impending; indeed she most firmly believed his own assertion that the unlucky words had broken from him without a moment of premeditation on his part.

But one thing grieved Marian deeply, and caused her a bitter sensation of remorse; she felt that in her inmost heart those words had not horrified her as they ought to have done; so far from seeking earnestly to obliterate them from her recollection, she knew and painfully owned that she was more inclined to cherish their memory than to strive with all the force of her will to banish them for ever from her mind.

This reflection caused her inexpressible bitterness; she felt as though she were guilty of treachery and falsehood towards Augusta, and she hated herself to think that she should for even an instant derive a base satisfaction from a confession, which if revealed to her sister, would be the means of inflicting on her the most intolerable anguish and humiliation.

Tossed and distracted by meditations of this uncomfortable nature, she lay for a long time awake; and was at length just on the point of dropping into an uneasy slumber, when she heard the door of her room softly opened, and looking hastily up to discern who the intruder might be, she perceived that it was her sister.

Robed in a long white dressing-gown, and carrying a small taper in her hand, Augusta, with her pale stern face and dark solemn eyes, presented rather an alarming spectacle to the startled gaze of the bewildered Marian. A far away remembrance dawned rapidly on her mind of a performance of "Lady Macbeth," which she had once witnessed; and something in her sister's air and manner vividly recalled the bearing of that merciless and ambitious woman, as she taunts her husband into the commission of the crime that dyed both their souls with blood.

Feeling rather nervous, Marian raised herself on her elbow.

"Is that you, Augusta?" she timidly inquired. "Do you want anything?"

"I am glad you are awake," replied Miss de Burgh, putting the taper on a table near the bed, and seating herself on a chair close to her sister; "for I wish to speak to you!"

"Oh, Augusta! if you would only not

look at me in that way," said Marian, shuddering. "I have not done anything to deserve this coldness from you!—I have not indeed!"

"I know what you have done—I know what you are doing, or rather trying to do," replied Augusta, laying one hand on the bed, and gazing at her sister with an expression of deep scorn and hatred; "you are seeking to win from me the love of one who is my plighted husband. You are laying yourself out to lure him with your treacherous face and your false eyes, and the sweet looks that you know so well how to assume——"

"Augusta! Augusta! you will kill me if you say such cruel things!" gasped Marian, almost inarticulately. "How can you accuse me of what would be the basest wickedness, such as I would die sooner than commit?"

"Hush!" replied Augusta, raising her finger as if in warning, and speaking in a low concentrated voice; "do you wish to alarm the house, and bring others to listen to my opinion of you? You cannot impose upon me, however much you may try to do so, and however you may choose to blind your own eyes to the consequences of the conduct you are now pursuing. You would have his mother too on your side;" here she laughed bitterly, and Marian shrank from her to the farthest corner of the bed. "You have beguiled her into thinking you a paragon of perfection; and no doubt she deeply regrets that she cannot have you for her daughter-in-law, instead of the unworthy individual who is expected to fill that enviable position."

"Augusta!" interrupted Marian, in a pleading voice, "you wrong Lady Agnes as well as me. Only this afternoon she spoke of you with the warmest interest and affection. It was in allusion to your future home that she entered into that description of Bellingham Court. She seemed to fear that a country life might be wearisome to you, after living so long on the Continent; and then she said she was persuaded a home so very lovely would more than atone for the loss of the variety to which you had been accustomed."

"She was really extremely considerate!" replied Augusta, with an undisguised sneer; "and I trust you felt able to reassure her mind on so very important a point. No doubt you convinced her that *you* would regard it as the summit of earthly felicity to pass the remainder of your days in such a home, and with such a husband, and, above all, with such a mother-in-law!" and again she laughed that harsh insulting laugh.

"Oh, Augusta! Augusta!" sighed Marian, clasping her hands together, "what have I ever done to you that you should speak to me like this? We are two only sisters—the children of one mother: surely we might have lived happily together—surely you might have loved me a little. I have never harmed you that I know of; and yet you say things to me that break my very heart! Oh, how I wish I had never left Summerton! I was happy there—everyone loved me and was kind to me; and I did not dream of the bitter trials that were in store for me here."

"Would, indeed, that you had remained at Summerton," replied her sister; "and it was all my own doing too, bringing you here. Your father would never have consented to receive you but for me. Fool that I was! dolt! idiot! to urge on him a scheme that has led to results like this! But listen to me: I give you one more warning. Do not seek to cross my path as you are now doing; leave me and my concerns alone, or you may yet live to regret the day when you wilfully thwarted me! You may bitterly rue the hour you first saw the shores of Italy!"

"But what have I done? What am I doing?" inquired Marian, piteously. "I will stay away from Lady Agnes Bellingham's if that is my crime."

"Going there is not a crime," replied her sister, coldly, "but you remained there under false pretences; you knew that Sir Charles intended dining at home."

"I did not—indeed, I did not," said Marian, eagerly; "Lady Agnes told me he was going out, and only then did I propose to remain."

"Then how came Sir Charles to stay at

home?" demanded Augusta, looking steadily at her sister.

The fixed gaze and the sudden remembrance of what had really caused the change in his intentions, as well as of the consequences that had resulted from it, brought a vivid blush to the pale cheek of Marian, which Augusta no sooner perceived than she haughtily remarked—

"There is no need to answer me; your guilt is plainly written on your countenance, though I knew it too well before. Say nothing more," she added, with a cold wave of her hand, as Marian strove to speak; "it will only be to unite falsehood of speech to falsehood of conduct. But we understand each other now," she continued, rising from her seat; "and you will do well to beware of such treachery for the future—if not, the consequences are on your own head."

So saying, without waiting for a reply, she turned away; and taking the taper from the table, went silently from the room.

For many a long sad hour Marian tossed on her sleepless pillow, her mind bewildered

and agitated by all she had passed through,
and her heart disquieted by emotions of the
keenest remorse, when she thought that
there might perhaps be some shadow of
truth in Augusta's accusation, that she had
indeed diverted her lover from his allegiance
to herself, and that such a result would never
have taken place if only Marian had continued to reside at Summerton.

The eager words that Sir Charles had so
unexpectedly addressed to her still rang in
her ears: even in darkness and solitude she
felt that her pulse beat quicker, and her
heart thrilled with pleasurable emotions
as her too faithful memory again recalled
them to mind. The next moment she
despised herself for doing so, and felt as
though her sister had not spoken more
harshly than she merited, when she called
her base and treacherous.

"Oh! that such words should ever be
applied to me—and perhaps applied with
truth!" sighed poor Marian to herself, as
she buried her weeping face on the pillow:
"am I indeed the wretch that she would

make me? Oh! surely, surely not! I did not know—I did not think that he would send that apology; but I *was* glad when he told me he had done so, and I think he knew I was—indeed I remember I said so —not dreaming that it might be wrong. Was it really wrong? Should I not have said so? It was soon afterwards that he said—what he did;" and all unseen as she was, Marian clasped her hands on her hot cheeks, as if to stay the crimson tide she felt rushing into them with the memory of that interview so indelibly impressed on her imagination.

For many a silent hour gloomy reflections chased each other through her wakeful brain; then came a time when they were gradually and confusedly blended together, and the power of coherent thought was merged in the unreasoning images of sleep.

She slept, and she dreamed; and this was her dream :—

A broad and beautiful river was flowing through a lovely landscape; shady trees lined its banks, bright birds fluttered about their branches, the sky above was blue, and an eternal sunshine was beaming over all.

She stood on the flowery bank, looking into the pure and pellucid depths; and it seemed to her that this river was the emblem of her own life.

Presently some one approached and came softly behind her; she knew who it was, and a glad smile overspread her countenance. Sir Charles Bellingham, for it was he, came and stood beside her; and, hand clasped in hand, they looked together into the glassy stream; when suddenly a dark shadow fell on sky and water, the sun disappeared behind threatening clouds, the leafy branches shivered, a low moaning sound was on the river; it was no longer calm, but dashed about in restless waves, that increased in violence at every moment.

Surprised and alarmed she turned to Sir Charles to inquire what had caused this change; but he was gone! and in his place stood Augusta, pale and angry, with a terrible expression in her eyes, from which Marian shrank in dismay—shrank step by step, as her sister came closer to her—shrank till she seemed to lose her footing on the crumbling bank, and in another moment she was struggling in the cold dark river. And Augusta looked on calmly and pitilessly, and stretched out no helping hand; nay, she walked by the side of the stream, and watched her sister floating helplessly down; and the glance of those stony eyes told Marian that from her no mercy was to be expected.

Then the white, rigid lips opened, and in a hard, cruel voice she spoke these words:— "I gave you full warning; I told you that you should bitterly repent the day you crossed my path: the time has now come, and you have met your fate. Hope for no aid from me!"

Gasping for breath, and in a wild agony of terror, Marian awoke; feeling as though the vision were a horrible reality, and her deadly peril even now hardly averted.

It was with great difficulty that she prevented herself from screaming for assistance, so vividly was her dream impressed on her mind.

But she did refrain; and in a minute or

two, reason and recollection came back to her, and she no longer dreaded to raise her head and look around.

Everything in her room was visible enough, for the first rays of dawn were forcing their way through the loosely-drawn curtains; and Marian sat up in bed and looked wearily round her, and felt a sensation of relief as her eyes fell on the familiar objects, telling her in very unmistakable language that she was safely and fully awake, and the images which even now caused her heart to beat were but the phantasmagoria of a fevered imagination.

While she gazed, the clock of a neighbouring church struck six; and as she listened to its slow resonant tones, there came into her mind an old superstition of her native county, and laying her tired head once more on the pillow she sank into a faint and fitful slumber, her lips still murmuring the words of one of her favourite ballads:

"I knew that the morning dream was true."

CHAPTER XIV.

WHEN the faithful Marshall entered the room of her young mistress and proceeded to undraw the window curtains, she found Marian buried in a slumber so profound that the various noises made by her attendant never once caused her to stir. This was so unusual a circumstance, that Marshall went up to the side of the bed, and then for the first time observed the fatigued and worn-out appearance of the young girl, the paleness of her cheeks, and the distressed expression of her countenance.

"Dear Miss Marian!" she whispered softly to herself; "how tired and sorrowful she looks, poor young thing! Very different she would look when I used to rouse her at Summerton; she was as blithe and cheery as any bird in those days; indeed, many's the time I have found her dressed and out in the garden when I went to call her." And the worthy woman sighed deeply as the remembrance of those pleasant home-days returned to her mind.

The increase of light had probably disturbed Marian; for while Marshall was hesitating as to the propriety of leaving her to finish her slumber, she suddenly awoke, and looked sadly and wearily about her.

"Do you think you should get up, Miss Marian?" suggested Marshall; "you don't look at all well this morning."

"I am quite well," replied her young mistress, quietly; "but I did not sleep very soundly, and I feel rather lazy in consequence. I shall feel better when I am up."

But if she felt better, she did not look so; and on descending to breakfast her heavy eyes and pallid cheeks aroused a general feeling of anxiety respecting her, which her depressed and languid manner did little to allay.

A riding expedition to visit some ruins

in the neighbourhood had been arranged to take place that day, and Mrs. Talbot at once laid a veto on all idea of Marian accompanying the others.

"Oh, grandmamma! may I not go?" she replied; "I feel as if the ride would do me so much good."

"No, my dear, it is far too long; you must not think of it for a moment. You know you have Lady A——'s party this evening; and if you wish to be at all fit for it, you must not fatigue yourself in the meantime."

Lady A——'s was to be a *tableaux* party on a very magnificent scale; and among those on whom the noble hostess was most prominently depending for assistance on the occasion, were the two lovely Miss de Burghs—their strongly contrasted style of beauty rendering them peculiarly valuable "subjects" in the combination of a group. Therefore, for the "brilliant blonde" of the programme to be looking pale and languid would be a most unfortunate *contretemps;* and when Marian more fully inspected her-

self in the glass, and remarked her colour-
less cheeks, and the dark circles round her
eyes, she shook her head, and owned reluctantly that grandmamma was in the right,
and it might be advisable that she should
reserve herself for the evening, and endeavour to recover at least a portion of her
usual roses. She was lying on the sofa in
the *salon* when Sir Charles Bellingham arrived to escort them in their ride. He cordially greeted the assembled party; and
Marian tried hard to make her reception of
him as frank and unembarrassed as usual,
though it was not very easy for her to do so,
feeling as she did, even without glancing in
that direction, that the keenly-observant
Augusta was narrowly watching every look
and action, and rigidly weighing each
syllable that fell from her lips.

" You don't look quite well, Marian," said
Sir Charles, kindly, as he advanced to shake
hands with her; "nothing wrong I hope?"

Marian was rosy enough now, and would
have given all she possessed to avert the
blush she felt stealing over face and throat,

and which she was certain would be instantly remarked by Augusta.

"I am a little tired this morning," she replied, faintly; "that is all."

"She did not sleep very well last night, and is looking like a ghost to-day," volunteered Mrs. Talbot; "so I am going to put her under lock and key till the evening, by which time she will, I hope, be quite herself again."

"Then is she not to ride with us this afternoon?" said Sir Charles, in a tone of disappointment.

"I think not," replied Mrs. Talbot; "it will be wiser for her to remain at home. She is not quite a Hercules you know, Sir Charles."

"I see you are dressed already, Augusta," remarked the young baronet, addressing his *fiancée*, "or I should have been inclined to suggest our postponing the expedition till Marian is able to accompany us. Had we not better do so?—we can ride in some other direction to-day."

"Oh, please don't!" interposed Marian,

eagerly; "I hope you will not alter your ride on my account. I can go there some other time."

Before she had finished speaking she regretted her impetuosity; for the hard cold look came into Augusta's face, and she set her lips firmly together for a moment, then she replied in an indifferent tone—

"Having dressed, I mean to ride; and having arranged.to go to Albano, I prefer doing so. I cannot veer about so easily as some people."

The last words were muttered almost as if to herself; but Sir Charles and Marian heard them, though no one else did. The hot blood mounted rapidly to Sir Charles's brow, and a hasty reply was on his lips; but with one glance at the downcast countenance of Marian, he checked himself, and turned away as if to avoid any further discussion.

At this moment Sir John de Burgh entered the room, and said that the horses had just come to the door—when Augusta instantly rose and announced her perfect readiness to start. Sir John was speaking to Mr. and Mrs. Talbot when Sir Charles turned round to say good-bye to Marian.

"I am so very sorry you can't go with us," he observed. "Do you really not feel inclined to postpone this excursion, Augusta? It seems to me such a pity to go without your sister."

"The ruins are not going to run away that I know of," replied Miss de Burgh, with difficulty maintaining an appearance of composure, though something in the tone of her voice told Marian of the storm raging within; "Marian may have a dozen opportunities of seeing them if she chooses. I intend going there to day!" so saying, she swept haughtily past him, and without another word or glance quitted the *salon*.

Sir Charles looked keenly annoyed, and Marian read his feelings of displeasure in his expressive countenance.

"Oh, Charles, go after her!" she urgently whispered ; "please go directly. I shall see the ruins some other time; don't keep Augusta waiting now."

"She is not so considerate towards others as to make one very anxious to consider her," replied Sir Charles, rather doggedly; "but I shall go—I am going, Marian," he added, seeing her look of unaffected distress. "I would do anything to please you."

And he proceeded downstairs to the courtyard in pursuit of Augusta, whom he found already mounted and engaged in an animated conversation with Count Salvi, who seemed to be going to ride likewise; for his horse was held by a groom at the door. Miss de Burgh took not the slightest notice of Sir Charles, who, after a rather distant bow to Count Salvi, was busying himself in examining the condition of the reins; but addressing her father, who was immediately behind him, she said in a calm distinct voice—

"I have asked Count Salvi to give us the benefit of his escort, papa. He knows the ruins well, and can point out all their most striking attractions."

"We are well off in having so excellent

a *cicerone*," replied Sir John, courteously; "and now, as we seem all ready, I propose we should start at once."

He proceeded to mount his own horse, and while he was doing so, Augusta lightly touched hers with her whip, and turned out of the courtyard, at the same time making a remark to Count Salvi, and thus necessitating his keeping closely by her side. Something in her manner of doing this struck the wily Italian, who had also observed the existence of a slight coldness between her and Sir Charles.

"Aha! something wrong here!" was his well-pleased mental comment. "A lover's quarrel! It is not at all my *métier* to cast oil on the troubled waters—I must rather lash them into further fury."

To which grateful task he accordingly very willingly devoted himself. The result was that Miss de Burgh retained him as her escort during nearly the whole expedition; and unless when the broad expanse of the *campagna* enabled them to ride abreast for a considerable distance, her attention and conversation were almost exclusively bestowed on Count Salvi.

Sir John de Burgh and Sir Charles Bellingham were therefore *tête-à-tête* companions for the greater portion of their ride; and the former during their return availed himself of the opportunity to broach to his future son-in-law a proposition that had for some little time past been seriously occupying his mind. After some few preliminary observations, he remarked—

"I have been reflecting upon your marriage with Augusta, my dear Bellingham, which at one time I decided had better take place in Italy—in Rome; but now I am inclined to think another plan may be more advisable."

"And that is——?" inquired Sir Charles, who did not particularly relish the discussion.

"To let it be celebrated in England, at the Abbey; that is, of course, if you have no objection to this arrangement."

"Not the slightest—in fact, I think I should prefer it so myself," said Sir Charles, cordially; for he felt a sensation of relief in the prospect of delay.

" I am very glad this plan will suit you," observed Sir John, internally a little sur-prised at the coolness with which his propo-sition of postponement was received. " You are aware," he continued, " that I have been for many years—in fact, for nearly seven-teen—an absentee from my own country and my own property. Painful circum-stances—the death of a much loved wife—led at first to this unwise proceeding, but at the time I was incapable of sober reflection. I have now come to the conclusion that it will be best to return to England, and take up my abode at the Abbey. I can see that Marian would much prefer this to a con-tinued residence on the Continent; and as I hope to retain her at least for some time as my companion, I feel anxious to gratify her inclinations as far as I possibly can. Sum-merton, her home for so many years past, is only a few miles distant from us; so it will scarcely feel like a separation from the kind relations who have brought her up—

and Bellingham Court is but half a day's journey from the Abbey, Augusta and you will, therefore, be within easy reach of us, and I trust we shall meet very frequently."

"I hope so, indeed," said Sir Charles, cordially; "it will always be a sincere pleasure to me to receive you and Marian as my guests at the Court: the more frequently you come, the better pleased we shall be."

Sir John bowed politely in reply.

"I am very glad to have had this little explanation with you," he continued; "I have been reflecting over it for some time. I shall inform Augusta of the proposed alteration in our plans, and of your perfect acquiescence in it. I have no doubt she will herself see how favourable an opening it presents for our return to a county we have so long deserted; the rejoicings attendant on the wedding will enable us to gather all our neighbours around us, and we shall in this manner resume occupation of the Abbey under the most favourable and brilliant auspices."

" And when?" inquired Sir Charles, with a little hesitation, "when do you consider it probable you may return to England?"

"Of course, I must be as accommodating as possible under the circumstances," replied Sir John, smiling; "and remembering the proverbial impatience—or is it *inconstancy?*—of lovers, I must shorten the ordeal as much as I can. Let me see. It is now nearly the middle of April, and the early part of May will find us in Naples; where I conclude we shall wish to linger for two or three weeks. After that, we shall make the best of our way home, arriving there I trust not later than the middle of June. Some necessary arrangements will then remain to be completed; those lawyers and milliners are such procrastinating characters, there is no getting out of their hands. Therefore I do not see how the wedding can well take place before the end of July, or the beginning of August; not a bad time, however—for if you are a keen sportsman, a lodge in the Highlands on a good grouse-moor would be an admirable idea for the honey-moon."

"A very good one, indeed!" replied Sir Charles, rather absently; for his thoughts were not exactly running on his honeymoon.

Just at this moment they were overtaken by Miss de Burgh and Count Salvi; and as the sky looked rather lowering, and a heavy shower seemed impending, the whole party accelerated their pace to a degree that for the present precluded all necessity for further conversation. Neither Sir Charles nor Augusta had been for an instant alone, either in going out or returning; so there had been no opportunity for any reconciliation since their little awkwardness at starting. They parted with cold formality, and no further intercourse took place between them till they all met in the evening at Lady A——'s. Augusta's manner was still chilling and distant—this nettled Sir Charles, who did not think he had given her any very serious ground of offence, and considered that he had a better title to feel aggrieved than she had, on account of her selection of Count Salvi as an

escort, and her thoroughly marked avoidance of himself.

So he determined to take no notice whatever of her studied coldness, but to pay her
off in her own coin; and he devoted himself
to doing the agreeable in a very general
manner, the larger share of his attentions
being reserved for Marian and Miss Crewe;
a proceeding that only tended to increase the
strong feeling of irritation already existing
in the mind of Augusta.

The party was a large and brilliant one;
and Lady A—— had summoned to her assistance several of the cleverest young artists
in Rome, who had willingly exerted their
taste and ability so as to dispose of the rich
materials placed at their command in the
most effective manner possible. The result
was a series of striking and exquisite pictures,
their subjects culled from all imaginable
sources, far surpassing both in design and
execution anything of the same nature ever
before witnessed in Rome.

The contrasted beauty of Augusta and
Marian de Burgh had been employed on

various occasions with charming effect; and one particularly excellent group had been arranged in which Sir Charles Bellingham was to appear as Richard Cœur de Lion, and Marian as his fair haired queen Berengaria; the subject being the well known scene when King Richard was stabbed by a poisoned dagger, and his heroic wife insisted on sucking the venom from the wounded arm.

Sir Charles made a very handsome representative of the lion-hearted monarch; and the ladies, knights, and various other figures grouped around were all well-chosen and skilfully arranged: but the most striking feature of the *tableau* was the fair Berengaria; and certainly if that much celebrated queen were only one half as beautiful as her youthful representative, she well merited all the praises bestowed upon her by contemporaneous history. So very lovely was Marian de Burgh's appearance in this character, that even those who knew her well were startled by her extreme beauty. The timidity by which it was evident she was all but overcome lent such a look of wild terror to her eyes, such a tenderly appealing expression to her countenance, that if she had been the most finished actress in the world she could not have performed the part more thoroughly. It was a crowning success; and loud and rapturous plaudits followed the final disappearance of the *tableau*.

To enable the performers in the various *tableaux* to see those in which they were not required, Lady A—— had caused a portion of the long gallery to be fitted up in such a manner that a most admirable view could be obtained from it. Orange trees and other flowering shrubs had been arranged in a semicircle on each side, so as not to interfere with the vision of the spectators in the rear, and yet to permit of an excellent look-out on the part of all behind the leafy screen, which was so constructed as to enable them to see perfectly without being in the slightest degree visible themselves.

Into one of those retreats, which was entered by a door leading from what Lady A—— called the " green-room," Miss de

Burgh retired from the bustle and noise around her, as her feelings were in a condition of excitement that peculiarly disinclined her for participation in the gaiety of the evening. From this seclusion she witnessed the *tableau* of " Richard and Berengaria;" and here she also became the unwilling auditress of a conversation carried on between two ladies in her immediate vicinity, who little guessed by whom their remarks were overheard.

"Oh! what a pretty creature!" exclaimed one of them, a new arrival in the Roman capital, as she raised her glass more minutely to inspect the kneeling Berengaria. "What a complexion! what hair! who is she?"

" Miss de Burgh," replied her companion; " and the gentleman who acts King Richard is Sir Charles Bellingham."

"Oh! I have heard of them," said the stranger; " they are engaged to be married, I believe. What a charmingly matched pair they will make—and he looks devoted to her."

" Then that is rather unfortunate," replied her companion, laughing; " for that young lady is not his *fiancée*—only her sister."

"Oh! dear, what a pity; they are so admirably matched that I feel quite disappointed there is a sister in the case. What is she like? a beauty too?"

"Some people consider her handsome," said the friend; "I, for one, do not. She has a very fine face and figure, but is terribly cold and proud.   That lovely little sister is far more charming in my eyes; and I have heard it said that Sir Charles rather repents of his bargain now when it is too late."

"I can quite believe that," observed the first speaker, again raising her glass, "for I am sure he looked as if he adored that pretty Berengaria.   Depend upon it they have all made a mistake, and the square people have got into the round holes."

The two ladies laughed, and then the conversation wandered to other subjects, and Augusta was left to reflect on what she had heard.

Her meditations, as might be expected, were anything but pleasant; and more than one *tableau* passed unheeded by her as she sat there silently musing on the remarks to which she had been a listener. Then came a summons for her from the "green-room," and very reluctantly she rose to obey it.

"Fair Rosamond," was the name of the succeeding representation; it included only her sister and herself; and under all the circumstances it really seemed as if it had been carefully selected with a peculiar appreciation of the features of the case. In the present condition of Augusta's mind it was not surprising that her mimic offer of death by poison or the dagger should be marked by a stern air of reality and a vividness almost horrible; and poor little Marian felt herself tremble all over as she encountered those awful eyes, bent on her with a look that painfully recalled her fear-ful and never-to-be-forgotten dream, and reminded her of all she had suffered on that terrible night, which even yet made her heart throb wildly when its images of horror en-tered but for a moment into her recollection.

The *tableau* over and her costume laid

aside, Miss de Burgh once more betook herself to her retreat among the orange trees, where she trusted to find the seclusion she so eagerly coveted. She seemed destined however to overhear disagreeable observations that evening; for a group of young men established themselves just in front of her position, and she was again compelled to become an enforced listener to remarks materially affecting herself.

"*Per Bacco!* what an actress Miss de Burgh would make," observed one of the party. "I never saw anything finer on the stage than her attitude and expression as Queen Eleanor. It made me creep all over, it was so real and lifelike."

"Poor little Rosamond was shaking in her very shoes," said another, laughing; "I don't wonder at it with such a pair of eyes looking into her very soul. I have my doubts as to whether those two sisters get on particularly well. I shouldn't wonder if Miss de Burgh had been pitching into her just before; the little thing looked frightened out of her wits."

"I could fancy Miss de Burgh had a deuce of a temper; she looks it all over," said a third, joining in the discussion. "My own impression is that Bellingham rather regrets his plunge, and would back out of it if he could do so with decency. He is not at all the fellow he was formerly, one can see that with half an eye. Ever since the younger Miss de Burgh came over from England he has been an altered man; no doubt whatever of the fact."

"Rather awkward to marry one sister and be in love with another," observed the first speaker, laughing. "However, something of the same kind has occasionally struck myself; I noticed that he looked mighty fond of her in the scene they were in together—what hair she has, by the way —she might appear as Lady Godiva."

"She is a regular little angel," remarked another; "I'd rather have her without a sixpence than her sister with all her immense possessions. Those queenly women may be very awe-inspiring and all that sort of thing; but for a wife I should prefer a sweet little rosebud, like the young one. He'll be a lucky fellow that carries her off. Hist! there's the bell again: Miss Crewe appears in the next *tableau* as a novice taking the veil, and I want to have a good look at that wonderful red hair of hers; let us go a little nearer the stage."

And they all hurried away to obtain a better position, once more leaving Augusta a prey to her truly miserable reflections.

And it had really come to this! This was the manner in which she and her engagement were now freely and familiarly discussed in Rome.

Sir Charles Bellingham was openly spoken of as regretting the step he had taken, as being willing to retrace it if he could do so with decency, and all this because she had not been content to leave things alone, but had with her own hands brought this misery on herself, by placing in his path one whom, but for this act of folly on her part, he never had seen or known.

A crushing sense of humiliation was the

first keen emotion that took possession
of her heart. To think that she—she, the
haughty, and hitherto unrivalled Augusta
de Burgh, should be forced to succumb to
the puny attractions and influence of her
almost child-like sister; a sister whom for so
long she had slighted and despised, and
whose pretensions, if considered as superior
or even as equal to her own, she would
unhesitatingly have laughed to scorn. Very
bitter were Augusta's reflections as she sat
there silent and lonely; passing in painful
review the many corroborative incidents
that seemed to prove only too clearly the
truth of the observations so lightly bandied
about among those careless young men.

For her, all the pleasure of the evening
was over, if indeed it had ever possessed any;
it was fortunate that the universal excitement
produced by the *tableaux* prevented that
measure of attention being directed to her
which might otherwise have been the case;
and when she was more especially exposed
to observation in taking part in the perfor-
mances, the marvellous strength of her iron

will carried her triumphantly through an ordeal in which a woman of a gentler nature and feebler resolution must inevitably have given way.

Miss Crewe and Count Salvi alone of all the assembled company arrived at a pretty distinct conclusion on the subject : for both remarked the constraint visible between Sir Charles Bellingham and Miss de Burgh, and their unusual avoidance of each other's society. To the latter it was a source of the most unfeigned satisfaction, as every pang that rent the heart of Augusta occasioned him the keenest pleasure ; but the warm heart of Emily Crewe was much distressed by the unmistakeable misunderstanding that had evidently taken place between the lovers, the cause of which she was at no loss to determine. Towards the close of this eventful evening she encountered Sir Charles Bellingham in a corner of the gallery. The young baronet looked annoyed and *distrait*, and his replies to Emily's observations were not always entirely to the point.

The shrewd Irish girl watched him narrowly, and longed to bestow on him a little friendly advice, of which it seemed to her he stood greatly in need.

"And why shouldn't I?" she mentally soliloquized, as she noted the perturbation distinctly visible on his usually frank and cheerful countenance. "Onlookers see the progress of a game better than the players themselves; he has got into a mess, poor unhappy fellow, and one course alone can extricate him from his difficulties; why shouldn't I point out that course to him, since he does not seem to see it for himself? If my advice does not suit him, why he can only leave it alone; my conscience, at all events, will be clear. No doubt Norah would call me a goose and tell me it was no business of mine. That may be—and yet, somehow or other, I feel that it goes against the grain to stand and look quietly on, while he knocks his head against a wall—when perhaps a helping hand might save him from the blow. I'll do it!" she suddenly and impulsively exclaimed; "*coûte qui coûte*, I'll risk it!"

"What will you risk?" said Sir Charles, with a smile, as her remark roused him from a reverie in which he was indulging. "Don't undertake anything very tremendous; or at least let me help you if you must do it."

"Well, I shall decidedly be all the better for your co-operation," replied Emily, slyly. "I have a little scheme on hand about which I especially wish to consult you. Can you spare me an hour or so to-morrow morning?"

"Command me for any length of time you choose," said Sir Charles, heartily; "I am proud to think I can be of the slightest service to you, Miss Crewe. Hitherto the obligations have all lain the other way."

"Very well," replied Emily: "come and see me as soon as you please after breakfast to-morrow, and I'll hold a solemn consultation with you."

"I'll be there," said Sir Charles, smiling, "all ready to bestow on you the soundest and most sapient of advice. Wont you give me an idea of the matter in hand, so that I might read up the subject a little beforehand?"

" No," replied Emily; " you must restrain your curiosity till to-morrow, for I shall tell you nothing about it previously. Fortunately it is not a subject that requires any especial amount of reading up."

" All the better for me," remarked Sir Charles; " and no doubt an unbiassed opinion is far superior to one only formed on the judgment of others."

" I am not so sure of that, Sir Charles; you know Solomon says, 'In the multitude of counsellors there is safety.'"

" Solomon made many mistakes in his life, Miss Crewe; and he had the honesty to avow this, which is not a very frequent proceeding."

" Goodnight, Sir Charles; I can't stop to discuss Solomon now, Norah is beckoning to me. Let us hope that some of his wisdom will fall to our share to-morrow, for my subject is an important one."

" I second your wish," replied the young baronet; " and now allow me to escort you downstairs; your sister is provided for, I perceive."

CHAPTER XV.

MISS CREWE SINGS A BALLAD.

Punctual to his appointment, Sir Charles betook himself on the following morning to the apartments occupied by Mrs. Greville and her sister; where he found Miss Crewe, seated in the drawing-room, evidently awaiting his arrival.

The young lady looked a little embarrassed, an unusual occurrence with her; but she shook hands very warmly with her visitor, and then motioned him to a chair close to that in which she had been previously seated.

" How very well everything went off last night," was her first remark; " Lady A—— may congratulate herself on a perfect success."

" Indeed she may," replied Sir Charles;

" the whole thing was admirable; but then she had most valuable or rather *invaluable* assistance from yourself and many other fair auxiliaries. The display of beauty was really dazzling; I don't know when I have seen so many pretty faces together at one time."

" Yes, I daresay there were," said Emily reflectively, " a good many *pretty* faces; but when the moon, or rather when two moons are shining, one does not look very much at the stars."

" That depends very much upon whom you call the moons and whom the stars," replied Sir Charles, laughing. " I make a stand for three moons at the very least; and Lady A——, to say nothing of half a dozen other acknowledged 'beauties,' wont thank you very much for classing them among the minor constellations."

" The two moons last night were the two Miss de Burghs, Sir Charles, as you very well know;" and Miss Crewe nodded her head with great decision.

And very brilliant and beautiful moons they were, " replied Sir Charles, smiling;

"but as I said before, there was a third moon, an Irish one, whose light was no less radiant than the others."

" Well, well," said Emily, shrugging her shoulders, "woman as I am, I never yet made a struggle for the last word; I never could see why that sin is always laid at the feminine door; I always find men infinitely more tenacious in holding to their opinions."

" I am perfectly ready to argue that point with you," said Sir Charles, laughing.

" Sure now be quiet, can't ye!" exclaimed Miss Crewe, putting on a delicious touch of the brogue, and holding up her hands in affected alarm. " Look here now, Sir Charles—" and a very becoming blush mantled her beaming countenance, while she raised her finger to her rosy lip and assumed an air of half comic perplexity; " I asked you to come here this morning for a particular purpose; and I begged that goodnatured sister of mine to keep out of the way, and let me have a comfortable *tête-à-tête* talk with you."

" I feel immensely flattered," replied Sir

Charles; "as from such an intimation I conclude I am about to assume the office of father confessor, and become the confidant of some deeply-interesting communication."

"What I am going to tell you is interesting enough to me at least," and Emily sighed, and a shade of sadness stole over the usually joyous features; "but I am not going to begin with that just yet. Some few preliminaries have to be gone through in the first place; one of them is that you must listen to a song."

"I shall be only too happy," said the young baronet, laughing; "and I trust all the other preliminaries are equally easy and pleasant."

"That remains to be proved," replied Miss Crewe, rising from her chair as she spoke. "Perhaps you may not like the song quite so much as you seem to expect. It is a ballad, and it has a moral." And she looked at him with rather a mischievous expression.

"I've conscientious objections to a moral being tacked either to ballads or novels," observed Sir Charles; "can't you omit it?

we'll take it for granted. Good people always happy; wicked people always wretched; there you have it at once."

"But that is not at all the moral of my song," replied Miss Crewe, "as you will perceive when you listen to it. It is the history of three people, about whom I expect you to be very much interested; and the moral is contained in all that they said and did, and is not specially added at the conclusion."

"That is a capital plan," said Sir Charles smiling; "because I am so remarkably thick headed, that perhaps if I don't look out very carefully for the moral, it may escape my notice altogether."

"Don't delude yourself with that idea," replied Emily, shaking her head; "you will see it very plainly indeed, as I intend that you shall do. In the first place however, you must promise me that you will listen very attentively, so as not to lose a single word."

"*Parole d'honneur*," said Sir Charles, laying his hand on his heart, "you shall be able to cross-examine me afterwards as rigidly as you like; I shall be well 'up' in the minutest particulars."

"Very well," replied Miss Crewe. "It is a Scotch ballad," she continued; "but the few Doric words that occur in it are very simple and easily understood. The gist of the story is plain enough; and it struck me that I could not find a better text for a little sermon which I am going to inflict on you afterwards."

"My dear Miss Crewe!" and Sir Charles raised his hands in affected horror; "first a moral—and then a sermon! Have a little mercy on me!"

"Hush! now listen," said Emily, smiling; "we'll discuss that point afterwards."

MISS CREWE'S BALLAD.

"There lived two sisters in a bower,
    Binnorie, O Binnorie!
The youngest was the loveliest flower,
    By the bonny banks o' Binnorie.

"There came a gay knight from the West,
    Binnorie, O Binnorie!
He loved them baith, but the youngest best,
    By the bonny banks o' Binnorie.

" He wooed the eldest to be his wife;
   Binnorie, O Binnorie!
But he lo'ed the youngest abune his life,
   By the bonny banks o' Binnorie.

" The eldest, she was vexed sair,
   Binnorie, O Binnorie !
And much envied her sister fair,
   By the bonny banks o' Binnorie.

" So it fell out upon a day,
   Binnorie, O Binnorie !
The eldest did to the youngest say,
   By the bonny banks o' Binnorie!

" ' O sister ! come to the sea-strand,
   Binnorie, O Binnorie!
And see the ships come safe to land,
   By the bonny banks o' Binnorie.'

" The youngest sat upon a stone,
   Binnorie, O Binnorie!
The eldest came and pushed her down,
   By the bonny banks o' Binnorie.

" ' O sister ! reach me but your hand,
   Binnorie, O Binnorie!
And you shall have one half my land,
   By the bonny banks o' Binnorie.'

" ' No, sister, I'll not reach my hand,
   Binnorie, O Binnorie !
For then I shall have all your land,
   By the bonny banks o' Binnorie.'

"' O sister! reach me but your glove.
     Binnorie, O Binnorie!
And you shall have my true knight's love,
     By the bonny banks o' Binnorie.'

"' No, sister, I'll not reach my glove,
     Binnorie, O Binnorie!
Then I shall surer have his love,
     By the bonnie banks o' Binnorie.'"

"There are several other verses," observed Miss Crewe, as she suddenly ceased singing, "but nothing more of importance to the story.   What do you think of it, Sir Charles?"

She looked up as she spoke, but she received no reply to her question; Sir Charles had his elbow on a small table beside him, and he leant his forehead on his hand, and remained so for several moments without uttering a word.

The silence was rather embarrassing; and Miss Crewe played a few bars of low soft music, waiting till her abstracted companion should have concluded his meditation.

"You are not angry with me, Sir

Charles?" she gently inquired, at the same time halting in her performance, and bending over towards him.

"Certainly not, Miss Crewe," he replied, with a deep sigh; "but angry perhaps with myself: I have been a great fool; I see it now, when it is too late."

"While there is life there is always hope," remarked Emily, cheerfully, "and I am not inclined to admit either of your propositions. You have heard my song—are you ready for my sermon?"

"Well — yes — I suppose so," said Sir Charles, with rather a grim attempt at a smile. "It wont have too many heads, will it?"

"What base ingratitude," replied Emily, in a gay tone; "when I am doing all in my power to serve you."

"Forgive me," said Sir Charles, sadly, "I fear I am making but a poor return for the interest you so kindly take in me; but if you only knew all, I am sure you would pity me."

"But I do know all," replied Miss Crewe,

"or at least I know enough perfectly to understand your case; and, believe me, I am extremely sorry for you, and I would fain help you to the utmost of my ability. Will you take me for your friend, Sir Charles—your true friend—who is ready to aid and advise you to the very best of her small power?"

As she spoke she extended towards him her little white hand, so soft and womanly; Sir Charles took it gratefully in his, and the gentle yet firm clasp seemed to speak to him of comfort and sympathy, and he mentally blessed the true woman's heart that had dared to break through the cold conventionalities of society, and offer him a friendship which, at the present moment, he felt to be his greatest need.

"Most gladly will I take you for a friend, Miss Crewe," he said, with eager warmth; "but there are difficulties connected with my position which you can never understand."

"Don't be too certain of that," replied Emily, smiling. "Irish women have a natural gift of shrewdness, and I may have a tolerably good guess at some of your present embarrassments. Does not my choice of that little ballad prove that I am somewhat behind the scenes?"

" Well—yes—in so far it does," said Sir Charles, dubiously, and a still more gloomy expression overspread his features.

" Then listen to me. Let me put the circumstances of the case plainly before you, and afterwards we shall see what can be done towards finding out a remedy. I did not send for you only to distress and tantalize you, and then coolly to leave you in the lurch. For some little time this course has presented itself to me; but it was only last night that I made up my mind to hesitate no longer. It may be foolish in me, Sir Charles, and it certainly is no particular business of mine; but I cannot bear to see so much unhappiness in store for those in whom I am so warmly interested, and not try to discover if it cannot by any possible means be averted."

" I fear it cannot," observed Sir Charles,

with rather a dismal shake of the
head.

"That we shall see," replied Miss Crewe,
decidedly. "One thing is very certain,
and that is, that much unhappiness exists
even now: of that fact, Sir Charles, you
must yourself be perfectly well aware.
You are far from happy—Miss de Burgh is
seriously annoyed—and Marian—poor little
Marian—*she* has had a very sad time of it
lately."

"All you say is only too true," said Sir
Charles; "but I can see no remedy that
would not be worse than leaving things as
they are. I have acted—not quite like a
fool perhaps—but certainly rashly. Now I
must pay the penalty, and submit—heaven
help me! as best I may."

"Time enough to talk of submission, Sir
Charles, when you have done all that a
man, all that a gentleman may. We have
a good old proverb in Ireland, ' 'Tis always
the darkest the hour before day;' let that encourage you. Things look rather black just
now, certainly, but ' Faint heart never won

fair lady;' there's another pithy saying for you; and a very fair lady is one whom you may perhaps win yet, if only you set about doing so in the right way."

"You would almost create a soul under the ribs of death, Miss Crewe," replied the young baronet, more hopefully; "but the prospect to which you allude is surely utterly impossible. I cannot in honour go back from my pledged word, nor will I do so."

"That is not the way to look at it, Sir Charles; there's an immense art in putting things properly. You have made a little mistake, not a very unusual occurrence in this blundering world of ours;" and the fair Irishwoman sighed. "Now the question is simply this : shall the consequences of that unlucky mistake cling to you for life? Or, on the other hand, shall you frankly and openly seek to retrieve that mistake? now—the sooner the better—before it is indeed too late."

"But how can I possibly retrieve my mistake?" inquired the young baronet, eagerly.

"In the only honourable way that is open to you," replied Miss Crewe, with flashing eyes and kindling cheeks, "by perfect straightforwardness and honesty! I am a woman, Sir Charles, and I know what it is to have loved!" and the long eye-lashes suddenly drooped, and tears gathered under the full, trembling lids: " and there never was a time when I would not have preferred my lover to have come to me frankly, and told me with his own lips that he no longer loved me, to discovering the fact from my own observation, slowly and painfully, and believe me, a thousand times more bitterly in the end. I have no very strong regard for Miss de Burgh, you know it; so it is not affection for her that makes me speak as I do. But from the very bottom of my heart I pity her for what she is now enduring; and in compassion to her I would urge you to end her sufferings, one way or another. Go to her this very day. Tell her that you mistook warm admiration and regard for love; and acting on this im-pression asked her to become your wife."

A faint groan from Sir Charles interrupted Miss Crewe in her harangue. She stopped, then finding that he did not speak, she continued; "no doubt the errand is not a particularly pleasant one, far from it; but think of the possible reward of your enterprise, and that will give you courage to proceed. Tell her all this; and then— then say that you have since discovered that another now occupies the position she once held, or you fancied she held, in your heart; and that you think it is neither worthy of yourself, nor of her, that you should continue the struggle of deceiving her, and that you have therefore resolved to throw yourself on her generosity, and tell her the whole truth, openly and without reserve. Now, I do not like Miss de Burgh, I frankly tell you so ; but she is not the woman I take her to be, if she does not at once release you from your engagement, and esteem you all the more highly that you have treated her honestly, and not feared her feminine weakness too much to be able to trust yourself to her nobility and

generosity of disposition. Some embarrassment—some pain—there must naturally be;
that is of course unavoidable; but believe
me, Sir Charles, it is sound advice I am
now giving you, and so you will find it in
the end."

She ceased speaking, and looked at him
eagerly and intently, hoping to read in his
countenance that he approved of her sugges-
tions and was disposed to carry them out.
But no! Sir Charles sat silent and dejected,
his eyes fixed on the floor, an air of gloomy
despondency clearly visible in his air and
manner.

"Oh! Sir Charles, I am so disappointed!"
said Emily, in a tone of slight vexation.
"I quite hoped to have persuaded you to
regard the matter from my point of view,
and I see you do not. And yet, I am so
firmly convinced it is the best, the wisest
plan."

"It would be so with some people, with
yourself, for instance," he replied; "but
with—with Miss de Burgh I do not feel so
sure of it. And then—as I told you before

—there are circumstances connected with the case that I cannot explain to you, which greatly increase my difficulty."

" I am not of a curious nature," observed Miss Crewe, " and I would not for a moment seek a confidence you prefer not to bestow on me; but I cannot imagine any circumstances which could militate against the wisdom of such a plan as the one I have just named to you."

" Did it concern myself alone I would be perfectly frank with you, Miss Crewe," said Sir Charles, hastily; "but others are involved as well, whose secrets I have no right to betray; on their account therefore I must observe a reticence on what would partly enable you to solve the enigma of my conduct."

" I always thought there was some dark mystery connected with his marriage," soliloquized the fair Emily, " and now I am quite convinced of it."

" Well, Sir Charles," she continued, addressing her companion ; " if my suggestion is one that cannot possibly be followed, then I can only say that I am extremely sorry for you; for you, and for those who must suffer along with you. But for the future your conduct must be very different. You cannot continue to act as you are doing now, or terrible misery will be the inevitable result. Much has been produced already; but it may not be too late to avert still more unhappy consequences. Pardon what may seem like impertinence, but I trust Marian is still ignorant of your unfortunate change of sentiments? You have never surely said anything rash to that poor innocent child?"

"I did not mean to do it," replied Sir Charles, rising and pacing the room in an excited manner; " but one unlucky evening I inadvertently said something of the kind."

Miss Crewe raised her hands in speechless dismay.

"I do not think Marian thoroughly understood me," continued the sorely perplexed young man. "What I said distressed her, and she begged me never to repeat such remarks; but I don't think

she fairly perceived all that they involved."

"I sincerely trust she did not," replied
Miss Crewe; "for I am sure such an idea
would cause the poor child a bitterer grief
than any she has yet known. Poor little
Marian! well for her had she never seen
the ill-omened shores of Italy."

"Were I to be the means of bringing any
sorrow or misfortune on her innocent head,
I should never forgive myself," said Sir
Charles hoarsely. ": Would to God I had
never seen her or known her! And yet to
think what might have been mine had I
only not—acted as I did," and again he
rapidly traversed the apartment.

"And can this bright vision never be
fulfilled?" said Emily, regarding him compassionately; "is that sweet Marian not
worth a struggle, even if it be a painful and
a difficult one? Oh, Sir Charles, think
well, think well, before you cast from you
such happiness as would be yours were she
your wife. Your .future—it may be hers
too—for ever blighted because of what can

be merely some punctilious feeling of generous honour; is it well to put aside the chance of winning Marian for such a sentiment as that?"

"The temptation is horrible," replied Sir Charles, with a gesture of despair; "but you do not know all—you cannot guess how I am situated."

Miss Crewe shrugged her shoulders, and inwardly felt a little impatience.

"Sir Charles," she remarked, in a tone of deep earnestness, "I cannot endure to see you casting away this chance; I will try to save you in spite of yourself. Surely the happiness of a life-time ought not to be so lightly perilled. Take warning by my sad experience. When I asked you to come here this morning, I had thought of telling you the history of my life, the history of an error in judgment, unwisely persevered in, that cost me every dream of my youth, every hope of my future—but I cannot do it. It is too sad a memory still: only if you could learn by experience, you would need no graver warning," and as she sat there the radiant head drooped low when she uttered those words, and the rich colour died out of the glowing cheeks; it clearly cost Miss Crewe no trifling pang to recal that episode in her past life.

"I owe you much," said Sir Charles, warmly; "very much, Miss Crewe, for what you have said already. Do not pain yourself by saying more; believe me the confidence you have bestowed on me is not ill-placed.   Would that I could return it by similar frankness: but I cannot—may not do so—or you would see how terrible is the temptation you hold before my eyes; you would also own that my conduct deserves pity more than blame, for between my present position and the happiness you tell me might yet be attainable, there is a great, an impassable gulf, which, did you see it, you would yourself allow honour forbade me ever to dream of crossing."

Miss Crewe shrugged her pretty shoulders, and put up her full rosy lip in token of incredulity. "Come now, Sir Charles, be reasonable, make up your mind one way or other, as you choose; but oh! for your own happiness and that of others, do it soon, immediately. As for this enigmatical *position* of yours, which may not be revealed to me, I can only say that I know of nothing that can exonerate you from the *sin*, for it is nothing less, of marrying and affecting to love one woman, while your heart is at the same time devoted to another."

"You are hard on me, Miss Crewe," replied Sir Charles in a despondent tone: " without a knowledge of the circumstances I assure you that you cannot judge me fairly."

" Well, I do not mean to say any more," rejoined Emily; " I have done my best, have said more than it was perhaps right or fitting I should say. But knowing how differently all the events of my life's history might have shaped themselves, had I only yielded to the words of prudent counsel, instead of being rashly governed by an imaginary theory grounded in folly and false pride and romantic impulses, it grieves me to see another entering on the same fatal path, and

I would fain stretch out a warning hand to stay you before it is too late, and you have taken any step that is irretrievable."

"I make you no promise, Miss Crewe, so far as regards my future course of action; but I shall at least most seriously meditate on what you have said to me. Many arguments will then I fear present themselves, even in addition to the potent ones you have yourself urged."

"Miss Marian de Burgh's soft blue eyes and heavenly smile to wit," replied Emily, laughing; "if they fail of convincing you, I must not wonder at the poor success of such feeble weapons as I have been able to wield. And now Sir Charles, I must really warn you off the premises, or we shall be getting into all manner of scrapes; we might have settled the affairs of a nation in this lengthy interview; I just trust it has not been so much valuable time and labour entirely thrown away."

Sir Charles took the hint and departed, after once more strongly reiterating his feelings of obligation and gratitude to his fair Mentor, and assuring her that her counsel should receive the most earnest consideration on his part, whatever might be the result at which he should finally arrive.

Their farewell was of the most friendly nature; and when the door had closed behind her visitor, and his retreating footsteps were no longer audible, Emily Crewe leant back in her chair and rested her blooming cheek on her dimpled hand, as she thought over the long and rather strange conversation she had just been holding, and wondered whether her forcible arguments would bear any fruit in the end, or whether she must for the future steel herself to look calmly on, and see the gradual consummation of the misery she had so eagerly laboured and striven to avert.

"I believe I am a fool for my pains," she muttered at length, giving a hasty toss to the rich waves of her tawny yellow hair; "but the fate of these people interests me strangely. There are times too, when I am tempted to doubt my disinterestedness—to mistrust the purity of my own motives—"

she was silent for a few minutes, and a frown
contracted the lovely forehead, just before
so frank and unembarrassed in its open
white expanse.

"Emily Crewe!" she exclaimed suddenly,
at the same time starting from her seat and
rapidly placing herself in front of a large
mirror suspended against the wall; "what
new and absurd folly is this? can it be
possible that *you* are false and treacherous—
a double dealer and a hypocrite? has Norah
been wiser than yourself when she said there
might be danger in all this friendly and
familiar intercourse?—have you allowed it
till it has become sweet and precious to you
—and have you been blinding your heart
all this time with the conviction that you
were his friend—nothing but his friend?
look into your own eyes that were wont to
speak the truth, and read there that your
suspicion is false—that you have not been
this base unworthy creature!"

She pressed her hand heavily on a marble
slab placed in front of the mirror, and she
leant forward and gazed long and steadily

into the clear depths of her bright blue eyes. Many sad thoughts crossed her brain as she stood there and looked earnestly at the beautiful vision reflected in the glass. Sternly and truthfully did she probe the inmost recesses of her heart; and suddenly a faint crimson tide began to surge over the fair countenance, which gradually deepened in intensity till Emily Crewe could no longer encounter even her own scrutiny, and the heavy lids drooped over her burning eyes, and she sank back into a chair and clasped both hands over her hot and tell-tale face, while tears of shame and wounded pride forced their way between her slender fingers.

"Fool! fool!" she softly murmured, "but ah! never did I dream of this! Is it to punish me for my conceit and rash self-confidence in slighting my sister's gentle warnings—saying as I did, that no danger existed for me, shielded by my sad and well remembered experience? Is it to prove to me that I am a poor foolish woman—weaker than the weakest—and in the very point

where I fancied myself so strong? Ah! me
—ah! me—and I have thought myself
qualified to give advice forsooth, and to
argue from the high ground of my superior
judgment! Emily Crewe! Emily Crewe!
you have fallen very low this day—you
have lost your own self esteem, the honest
approval of your own conscience! But all
is not lost yet," and she raised her tear-
bedewed countenance, while a bright glow
of noble resolution lighted up her speaking
features; "I will be true to myself, to the
instincts of my own better nature—I will
be their firm friend still. *Courage, mon
ami!* our watch-word may yet be 'victory'."

END OF VOL. II.